I0788419

THE SERPENT'S DRUM

WHISPERS OF A FORGOTTEN PAST

Asar Adewale Farid

TABLE OF CONTENTS

FOREWORD

By Scott Mays

It was a warm, sunny day in July 2019 when our paths first crossed, though looking back, I now realize it was God who brought us together in each other's lives. I had just moved from New Hampshire to Washington, D.C., still grieving the recent loss of my father in Philadelphia, my hometown. It was a season of transition, of divine pruning.

We met during the earliest days of building something special, an all-Black STEM teaching community, a high school that would grow to become our home for the next six years. It was the first time I had seen an entire staff of Black educators in one space: brilliant minds, deeply rooted in purpose. Our motto was "Team and Family," and it was more than just words; it was the truth we lived every day.

In that sacred space, I met my brother in spirit, Farid. I taught math, he taught science, but our conversations quickly grew far beyond the classroom. We spoke of God, of politics, of manhood, of being Black and divine in a world that often forgets it. Although I was practicing Buddhism at the time, they affectionately called me "Preacher" for the way I opened our morning meetings with rhythm and reverence.

However, it was Brother Farid who helped draw me closer to Christ, challenging and stretching my understanding of who Jesus is in my life.

In the quiet hours, we became co-authors of each other's journeys, offering feedback and encouraging one another through the long process of writing and releasing our first novels. In all of it, God was present. Strategic. Loving. Intentional. When I asked Him for help, He answered with presence, with people, with purpose.

And now, this book.

The Serpent's Drum: Whispers of a Forgotten Past is more than a story; it is a remembering—a sacred reclaiming of origin, faith, and divine power. Through Queen Eshe's bold voice, through the grace of her grandchildren, through the ancient rhythms carved into the serpent's skin and the Baobab wood, we are drawn back to a time before time. To rituals, to reckonings, to the first breath spoken into dust.

This tale is creative yet rooted, mythic yet intimate. It reimagines the Genesis story not to rewrite it, but to deepen it; to show a Creator not distant, but close. It invites us to see ourselves in the lineage of greatness, of brokenness, of redemption. It asks us: What does it truly mean to be saved? It reminds us that through Jesus, the ultimate sacrifice, we are reconnected to God without intermediaries, without rituals soaked in blood, because He became the blood that reconciled all things.

This book is not for the faint of heart. It is for the seeker—the one hungry to hear the whispers of ancestors and the heartbeat of the divine. The drum still speaks—and if you listen closely, you just might remember who you really are.

Welcome to The Serpent's Drum.

Scott Mays

Father, Leader, Educator, Author

CHAPTER 1

"A FAMILY HEIRLOOM"

"Do I hear five hundred thousand? Is that a bid, sir?" The curator's voice cut through the room, playful yet sharp, slicing the tension. "Don't be shy!" he teased, eyes scanning the audience. "Five hundred and fifty thousand on my right! Do I hear six hundred thousand? Yes!" His voice snapped like a whip, propelling the auction onward. "Six hundred thousand to the gentleman in the white suit!" he announced, excitement clear in his tone.

"Going once," the curator surveyed the room, anticipation thickening the air. "Going twice. Any bids for six hundred and fifty thousand?" His gaze searched the audience intently for any sign of movement. Silence. "No bids at six hundred and fifty thousand?" The room held its collective breath as the curator paused, fingers twitching above the gavel. The seconds dragged. Finally, decisively, he struck the gavel down with a sharp crack.

"And sold!" he declared, his voice ringing with finality. "To the fine gentleman in the white suit for six hundred thousand dollars!" The words settled over the room like the closing of a grand performance, and the crowd exhaled as if releasing a collective breath.

"The famous 18th-century cello, once owned by Napoleon himself, has been sold." The guests erupted into applause, congratulating the new owner on the prestigious acquisition.

"And now, for the star of the evening, appearing now on block number 55—the infamous Serpent Drum."

"If she would make her appearance on the turntable. A certified masterpiece of the golden age."

A delay of approximately three minutes occurred during the unveiling, caused by a malfunction in the storage tag. Behind the scenes, thirty-three workers scrambled to ensure the evening's sales proceeded smoothly. The anticipation in the museum thickened, as this was the final and most coveted item of the night. The Serpent Drum had been shrouded in legend for centuries, its origins rumored to date back to the dawn of humanity. Many doubted its existence, dismissing it as myth, while others were enthralled by the supernatural lore surrounding it.

Meanwhile, at the Freeman family home, relatives had gathered upon hearing that Grandmother Eshe was nearing her final moments. She lay peacefully in her bed, surrounded by loved ones who had come to bid her farewell. Her given name was Queen Eshe Freeman, bestowed upon her in honor of an ancestor from nearly a century ago. She had been lovingly bathed in fragrant oils from the motherland and dressed in flowing white garments, prepared for her transition. Incense filled the air, while flickering candlelight cast a warm glow, creating a serene atmosphere. Prayers were whispered at her bedside as family members touched her hands and gently rubbed her arms, honoring her journey.

With tears in their eyes, the family knelt at her bedside as Eshe motioned for them to come closer to her weakened frame. For the first time in weeks, she had gathered enough strength to speak. Were these to be her final words? The family watched nervously as she parted her lips, gasped for breath, and, with a raspy tone, declared, "Can someone pass me the goddamn remote? Jeopardy is about to come on, and y'all are in the damn way!"

The room erupted in laughter as someone quickly handed her the remote. "I'm not going anywhere yet," she exclaimed. "I'm waiting to see my babies one last time before I go. Trust me, when it's my time, I'll let you sons of bitches know! Now, somebody bring me a couple of those beers from the fridge!"

Grandmother Eshe had celebrated her 99th birthday just three months prior. She was wise, sharp, and full of life—and she was also fluent in profanity. More than her knowledge and wisdom, she had a gift for lightening any mood, easing the burdens of those around her with humor and blunt honesty. No matter the situation, Grandmother Queen Eshe was the kind of woman who spoke her mind without a filter, and if her words stung, so be it.

She lay in bed watching back-to-back episodes of Jeopardy, as if the show had given her a renewed sense of purpose. With a cold six-pack of Coors Light at her bedside, she shouted at the TV, fully engaged in the game.

"Who is George Washington, asshole!" she yelled, pointing at the screen. "Why the hell are you even on this show? You big dummy, don't you know George Washington crossed the Delaware River?"

Her family sat behind her, shaking their heads and clutching their stomachs with laughter. Though she kept them entertained, she knew her time was drawing near. She silently prayed that her two favorite grandchildren, Ibrahim and Issabella, would return soon. She was holding on for one last story—a story so powerful it could change everything.

Her breathing grew shallower, and her heartbeat was weaker than it had been the day before. "Lord, let me hang on till my babies get here, please," she whispered.

Meanwhile, while the rest of the family remained by Eshe's side, Ibrahim and Issabella sat among the audience in a packed auction hall. The room was filled with wealthy collectors, all eager to claim antique musical instruments. But Ibrahim and Issabella had a singular mission that night—to acquire a rare instrument, one that Grandmother Eshe herself had requested.

She had spent their childhood filling their minds with stories about this special drum. She had told them, time and again, that the drum was not just an artifact—it was their birthright. Some of her tales had seemed so impossible that they couldn't be real. But whether or not they believed in the legends, they were determined to fulfill their grandmother's wish. The drum would be her parting gift.

On this grand evening of refinement, Ibrahim stepped into the spotlight, his presence commanding admiration from every corner of the room. He was dressed in a suit of the deepest blood-red hue, so rich and striking it seemed to radiate energy. Under the ambient glow of the chandeliers, the material caught the light just enough to accentuate its luster, while sleek black stripes ran down the sides of his impeccably tailored trousers, adding an extra touch of distinction.

Beneath his jacket, he wore a crisp white shirt, freshly pressed and perfectly fitted, its pristine surface providing a bold contrast to his striking suit. The sharp collar framed his strong jawline, enhancing the air of quiet authority he carried. His matching jacket, expertly tailored to complement his frame, rested with effortless precision on his shoulders, elevating his stature and lending him an undeniable air of sophistication.

Adding a touch of personality to his ensemble, Ibrahim had chosen a neatly folded green pocket square, artfully tucked into the right side of his tuxedo jacket. The vivid green stood out against the deep red, a bold yet tasteful choice that infused his look with charm and individuality. As he moved through the room, the pocket square subtly caught the light, drawing admiring glances and further cementing his impeccable sense of style.

With every step, Ibrahim exuded confidence and poise, embodying the essence of classic elegance. He was not merely another guest at the gathering—he was a presence, leaving an indelible impression on all who had the privilege of witnessing his refined grace that evening.

Issabella was breathtakingly dressed, a vision of elegance and poise. She dazzled in a flowing green and white gown, the fabric catching the light as she moved. A deep yellow headdress adorned her head, covering her natural red locs, which cascaded down to her hips and were wrapped into an intricate crown. The train of her gown trailed three feet behind her, adding a regal air to her entrance.

Heads turned as she glided through the room, her presence drawing admiration from every corner. With each step, the soft material of her gown brushed against her skin, accentuating her figure with effortless grace. Her locs, rich and vibrant, framed her face like a halo, adding to the striking image she created.

The delicate scent of jasmine lingered in her wake, drawing people closer, their gazes fixed on her. Her eyes, deep and expressive, shimmered like stars against the night sky, carrying a quiet mystery that invited curiosity. A warm smile played on her lips, effortlessly radiating charm as she engaged in conversation.

As she moved, the atmosphere seemed to shift; murmurs and laughter filled the air, but it was her undeniable presence that held everyone's attention. It was as if time itself slowed, allowing all to take in the elegance of her movements and the warmth she exuded. In that moment, she was more than just a woman—she was a force of beauty and grace, leaving a lasting impression on everyone fortunate enough to witness her that evening.

Issabella earned her medical degree with a focus on DNA sequencing from Harvard University. During her time there, she graduated at the top of her class and served as president of the country's DNA Scientists Association. In addition to her academic achievements, she received numerous awards and was a leading figure in her field. Outside of science, she was also the lead singer in her twin brother Ibrahim's R&B band, Son of the Morning.

Ibrahim, her twin, was both the drummer and backup vocalist for their band. He earned his Ph.D. in Vibrational Analysis from Howard University, where his groundbreaking dissertation explored the relationship between music, sound frequencies, and their potential to heal the human body. His research focused on how specific musical instruments could produce vibrations capable of generating powerful energy, possibly aiding in recovery from illness.

As they sat in the crowded auction hall, waiting for the bidding to begin, Ibrahim turned to Issabella. "Do you remember the story Grandma told us about the drum with special powers?" he asked.

Issabella's eyes lit up with excitement. She nodded, then began recounting the tale—the story of a drum carved from the strongest African wood, coated with the dark black scales of a serpent's skin, and marked with streaks of red from the serpent's blood.

Their grandmother, Eshe, had inherited this legend from the days of slavery, passing down its significance and the identity of the drum's mysterious creator. As the auction progressed, Ibrahim and Issabella sat patiently, waiting for the moment they had anticipated. Then, at last, it appeared—the Serpent Drum.

The announcer spoke of its history and estimated age, but none in attendance truly understood the drum's origins, the secrets it held, or the blood woven into its past. The crowd stared in awe. The drum stood upright, solid and imposing, its presence commanding attention. Crafted from the sacred Baobab tree, it was coated in a red substance that bore an uncanny resemblance to blood, just as Grandmother Eshe had described. Embedded within its surface were the dark, scaled remnants of a serpent's skin.

All eyes remained fixed on the drum, captivated by its mystique. Since childhood, Eshe had told Ibrahim and Issabella that only a few shared knowledge of this drum outside their bloodline. She had spoken of its significance, whispering to them that the very snakeskin used in its construction was the same that Shekhinah had once used in the redemption of man.

Now, the drum sat prominently on the display stage, a focal point of the auction. Its top, covered in weathered snakeskin, gleamed under the harsh lights, where countless hands had once struck to create powerful rhythms. The paint shimmered beneath the bright auditorium lights, its colors vivid, pulsing as if alive. Every band and clasp remained perfectly intact, as though untouched by time, preserved for centuries.

It stood there, silent, yet heavy with history, beckoning wonder and speculation from all who gazed upon it. And now, the moment had arrived. The twins' hearts pounded, their palms slick with sweat. They clasped each other's hands, knowing this was one of the most defining moments of their lives. The anticipation in the room was electric. Tonight, the Serpent Drum was poised to become the most expensive musical instrument ever auctioned.

The music came to an abrupt halt, plunging the room into a heavy silence. Every eye turned to the stage, where the legendary drum, crafted from the hide of a serpent, stood, awaiting its fate. The tension was thick as the first bid was called. Then, the frenzy began. "Do I have a million?" The auctioneer's voice rang out, sharp against the hush. "Yes! Do I have 1.5 million?" The numbers soared. Each bid came faster, more desperate than the last. The room became a battlefield of wealth and willpower, a blur of raised hands and urgent voices, each competitor determined to claim the coveted prize of the evening—the Serpent Drum. For twenty relentless minutes, the bidding war raged. The stakes climbed higher, each offer outpacing the one before it. No one was willing to back down. Then, in a moment that cut through the chaos like a blade, Ibrahim and Issabella stood together, their voices rising above the storm.

"Five million!" they declared in unison. Their bid shattered the auction's rhythm. The room fell into stunned silence. No one else dared to challenge them. The Serpent Drum was theirs.

"Congratulations to the winners in my center section, holding card number 357!" the auctioneer announced, his voice crackling with excitement.

The room erupted in applause, a wave of admiration and disbelief sweeping through the crowd. The twins—still absorbing the magnitude of their victory—stood frozen in stunned silence. The legendary drum was now theirs. The air buzzed with energy, a tangible force thick with anticipation. They had just secured a relic of immense value, a treasure etched into history.

The applause grew louder, echoing off the walls as the weight of the moment settled over them. The drum, steeped in ancient mystery, was finally in their hands.

As the final gavel struck, marking the end of the auction, the drum was placed in their grasp. But its significance was heavier than its physical form—it carried the weight of destiny, of history, of a legacy passed down through generations. Ibrahim and Issabella exchanged a look, a silent understanding passing between them. The thrill of their victory surged through their veins. This was no ordinary acquisition—it was a piece of history, and it now belonged to them.

A bittersweet triumph consumed them, a mix of exhilaration and unease. Their hearts swelled with pride—this was the legacy Grandmother Eshe had entrusted them with, the sacred drum she had implored them to protect. It was finally in their possession, just as she had wished.

Yet beneath their joy, a storm of uncertainty brewed. The drum carried more than history—it held secrets, power, and perhaps even danger. What stories lie buried within its surface? What forces had they just unleashed?

As their driver sped through the night, the city lights stretched into streaks of gold and white, while the quiet suburban streets blurred past in a haze of urgency. The twins clutched the drum between them, its presence pressing heavily against their chests—not just in weight, but in meaning. They couldn't shake the fear creeping into their hearts. Were they too late?

Would they reach home before Grandmother Eshe transitioned to the ancestors, as she had so often spoken of in her final days? The urgency was suffocating. The responsibility they carried felt both like a blessing and a burden. Every ticking second stretched into eternity as they raced toward home, praying she was still there, still waiting for them, still holding onto the final thread of their family's story before it unraveled forever.

The drum was said to possess powers—an ancient force capable of healing any ailment when struck in a precise rhythm. Its secret was locked between them, understood only by the direct descendants of Queen Ayisha. No one outside their bloodline knew the true purpose of the Serpent Drum, nor the knowledge it held.

For generations, the story of the drum and the tragic events that led to their ancestors' enslavement had been passed down, a legacy of pain and resilience. Now, as the drum rested in their hands once more, a wave of pride swelled within them. This was more than an artifact— it was a victory. Issabella and Ibrahim had reclaimed their birthright, restoring the heirloom to its rightful place.

The wheels of the Bentley screeched as the driver took a sharp turn past the exit sign near the Freeman estate. Ibrahim and Issabella were almost home. The anticipation was palpable in the air as they prepared to present Grandmother Eshe with the family heirloom—an artifact that had been lost to their bloodline for centuries. As the car pulled up to the family estate, the grand iron gates, emblazoned with Freeman's Place, creaked open. The driver wasted no time, accelerating down the long driveway toward the house.

As the twins walked into the house, they headed straight to the room where Their Grandmother, Eshe, lay resting. They entered quietly and knelt beside her bed. "Grandmother, how are you feeling?" Ibrahim asked gently. Eshe, her voice soft but unwavering, gave a slight smile. "I'm a lot better now that you and your brother are here."

"Have you retrieved the drum as I requested?"

"Yes, ma'am," they answered in unison. "Good," she nodded. "Now pass me my last beer, and after I finish, we'll handle our business." Issabella glanced around and spotted five empty Coors Light cans crushed beside her grandmother's pillow.

Her eyes widened. "Grandmother, did you drink all these beers?" Eshe let out a raspy chuckle. "You goddamn right I did!" She held up the last can and smirked. "You want some of this one? It's real fucking good. This is the last one!" Issabella shook her head, suppressing a laugh. "No, ma'am. You go ahead and enjoy."

Grandmother Eshe quickly finished her beer and placed the crushed can with the others beside her bed. "Can you all be excused from the room?" she requested. "I need time with my favorite grandchildren, just for a little while."

As the family exited, Eshe sat up briefly, taking several deep breaths. Holding Ibrahim and Issabella's hands, she quietly said, "It's almost time now. My time on this plane of existence is coming to an end, but I know both of you are already aware of that."

"Grandmother, isn't this supposed to help you?" Ibrahim asked.

"No," Eshe replied. "This isn't about healing me. It's about setting right the wrongs that have affected us all."

Ibrahim and Issabella exchanged puzzled glances.

"Before I go, I must tell you a story—one passed down for generations before you. Until now, it was merely a tale, but you must understand that it is more than that. It is a prophecy about you, our family, and our connection to the Originator of the heavens and the earth."

Issabella and Ibrahim stood frozen, shock carved into their faces, their minds spinning with confusion. The gravity of the moment settled upon them—for they, and only they, had been chosen. Bound to fulfill a prophecy that stretched across time, they stood at the precipice of something far greater than themselves.

Grandmother Eshe, frail and fading, coughed weakly, her body surrendering to the passage of time. Her transition was near, the hour slipping away.

"Before it is too late," Eshe rasped, her voice barely above a whisper, "let me tell you a story..." She drew a deep, labored breath, her gnarled hands reaching for theirs, pulling them close. "This tale, my children, is unlike any you have heard before. Listen carefully, for the truth I speak tonight is ancient and unshaken, while what you've been told all your lives is nothing but a lie—a veil of deception. What I speak now... is the truth." Her voice softened further, each word fragile yet powerful.

"In the beginning... there was nothing. Only darkness. And then, the Creator spoke."

CHAPTER 2

"AN ELOHIM NAMED SHEKHINAH"

And after the Creator spoke, there was darkness. Then, there was Light. Once the Light emerged by His command, it filled the void, and from this sacred radiance, He shaped the heavens and the earth. With precision beyond human understanding, the Creator established seven levels of heaven.

As time unfolded, His presence expanded across the vastness of the universe. From the purest light, He called forth the Elohim, followed by the Jinn, forged from fire. But after the twelve Elohim were formed, the Creator turned His thoughts toward something far greater—a creation that would surpass all others.

He envisioned an Elohim who would not only serve Him with unwavering devotion but would also possess a gift unlike any before—free will. And so, in His infinite wisdom, He conceived the thought, spoke the word—and it was done. Shekhinah was born, the greatest of all His angels.

Shekhinah was more than beautiful; she embodied purity and perfection itself. A being of unfathomable power, she commanded the reverence of all who beheld her. Adored by the Creator, cherished by the Elohim, and respected by the Jinn, she stood above all.

On the third and fourth days, the Creator formed the sun, moon, and stars, each to shine in its own way and glorify Him. In their wake, the Kingdom of Ekiku emerged—a land crafted in honor of the Creator. Ekiku was a place of abundance, a realm of unmatched beauty and strength—an Eden, blessed with everything its inhabitants could desire.

The beings of Ekiku were neither Elohim nor Jinn—they were something else entirely. Supernatural entities with the power to shift their forms at will, soar through the skies, command the elements, and communicate with the very essence of existence. At the Creator's summons, they could move freely between Ekiku and the Kingdom of Heaven.

Abu Ogun, chosen by the Creator Himself, was appointed ruler of this sacred kingdom, entrusted with the task of bringing forth new life to inhabit it. To ensure his creations remained faithful to the Creator's will, Shekhinah, in all her splendor, was given the solemn duty of watching over him and his work.

Eager to fulfill the Creator's decree, King Abu Ogun sought to expand the kingdom—to claim the Earth and shape it into a reflection of Ekiku. Yet when he beheld the Earth, he found it desolate—an endless expanse of water, devoid of beauty and life. It bore no resemblance to the paradise of Ekiku.

With unwavering resolve, Shekhinah devised a grand plan to reshape the Earth in Ekiku's image. She presented her vision to King Abu, and with his full approval, the transformation began.

On the first day, Shekhinah parted the waters, revealing dry land. The oceans withdrew, making way for life to take root. On the second day, she adorned the land with towering trees, lush forests, and vibrant plants, all aligned with the Creator's will. On the third day, creatures of all kinds emerged, filling the earth with movement and purpose. On the fourth day, birds and winged creatures took to the skies. In just five days, the Earth, once barren, was now brimming with life.

But on the sixth day, as Shekhinah looked upon her creation, a stirring grew within her. A desire for something new took root—something unlike anything that had come before. She longed to shape a being with the freedom to think and act, not just to serve but to worship the Creator with love and devotion.

She brought her vision to the Creator, who, pleased by her idea, granted His blessing. With renewed purpose, Shekhinah returned to Earth and shared the news with King Abu. Together, they formed a new being—one fashioned from divine light and the dust of the earth. He would be called "Audam," a creation made in the likeness of the Creator.

Yet, Shekhinah's heart was still unsettled. Audam was incomplete. He needed a companion, someone to stand beside him, to share the responsibility of caring for the earth. She envisioned a woman, a counterpart to Audam, equal in purpose and strength. Her name would be "Lilith." And so, she was brought into existence.

On the seventh day, Shekhinah breathed life into Audam and Lilith. As they awakened from the void, awareness filled them, bringing understanding of their gifts, their purpose, and the language bestowed upon them by the Creator Himself. Around them, the world—a paradise in its purest form—awaited their hands, their care, and their devotion.

Audam, with a firm and deliberate hand, named the creatures, brought order to the world, and followed the Creator's silent directive. Lilith, in quiet devotion, tended to Eden's trees, always in communion with the unseen presence of the Creator.

Shekhinah, watching from the shadows, allowed herself a moment of quiet satisfaction—her work was complete. But even she, divine and tireless, felt the burden of creation and withdrew to the Kingdom of Heaven to rest.

Yet, as the Earth thrived under the care of Audam and Lilith, an unseen force stirred beneath the surface, and the true design of the Creator—hidden within time itself—began to take shape.

Grandmother paused, breathing heavily, as though the impact of her words still echoed in the room. Her voice grew softer. "Grandchildren," she said, her tone nearly prophetic, "I've only just begun the story. Listen closely, for the drum—the key to everything— is rooted in this ancient beginning. There is only one God, and to His name be all the glory."

The air was thick with tension, her words suspended like a curtain as they waited for the next revelation.

CHAPTER 3

"PRELUDE TO A DREAM"

The thick, musty southern air split apart with the sharp crack of gunfire. Rifles thundered behind her, sending bullets screaming through the air, hissing past her ears with deadly precision. Each shot sliced through the morning fog—a chilling reminder that death was just a breath away. But she didn't stop. She couldn't. Every muscle burned, begged for relief, but her body kept moving, faster, harder, driven by the sheer will to survive.

In the deep woods, birds scattered in a frenzy, startled by the furious barking of hounds charging eastward, their noses locked onto her scent. "You can't run, nigger! I'm gonna catch your black ass!"

The cruel voice cut through the dawn, mingling with the dogs' snarls and the sharp crack of gunfire. The shots rang out in quick succession, the bullets tearing through the air, so close they carried the whisper of death itself. Still, she ran. Gunshots cracked behind her, sending bullets streaking past her head, stirring the damp morning air with deadly precision. Her lungs burned, but she swallowed the pain. The plantation was far behind her now—the men, their rifles and whips, the snarling dogs—fading into the distance like ghosts. She wasn't just running for freedom. She was running to protect something far more precious than her own life. She carried a secret—one that, if discovered, could destroy everything.

Her feet pounded through the underbrush, the world around her a blur of darkness and shifting shadows. Towering pine trees loomed overhead, their jagged branches clawing at her bare skin, leaving behind thin trails of blood. But she didn't feel the sting—there was no time for pain. She had to keep running. She had to keep going. She plunged deeper into the woods, the thick scent of damp earth and pine filling her lungs. Her heart pounded, a frantic drumbeat in her chest, as she threw herself to the ground. Mud. She rolled in it, desperate to smother her scent before the hounds closed in. The cool, sticky muck clung to her skin, matted her hair, but she didn't care. It was a small price to pay for a chance to stay hidden. An opportunity to stay alive. Staggering to the riverbank, she gasped for breath, her body shaking with exhaustion. The rushing water called to her, cold and untamed, and she plunged her face into it, drinking deeply, desperately. The chill offered a fleeting moment of relief, but she knew it wouldn't be enough. Not with the dogs drawing closer, their howls slicing through the trees, their hunger sharpening with each passing second. Then, the sound of them. The dogs. Growling. Howling. Closer. Too close. She could hear their claws scraping against the dirt, their snarling throats raw with the thirst for blood. She had to move.

Her body shook, but she forced her legs to move, pushing forward into the thick brush. Her chest burned, her heart hammering against her ribs, but she kept running. She could hear them now—snapping jaws, pounding paws, the hounds closing in fast. Every step was a battle, every breath a fight. Her lungs ached, her body trembled, but she couldn't stop. The dogs were relentless, closing in like a storm. She couldn't outrun them—not for long. But she ran anyway. She ran for her life. She ran for the secret she carried, the secret that could destroy everything. Her legs moved with the desperation of a woman with nothing left to lose—but everything to protect. She tore through the dense woods, the jagged branches of pine trees clawing at her bare skin, leaving behind thin trails of blood. She didn't flinch. There was no time for pain. Dropping to the ground, she rolled through the mud, smearing it over her arms, her legs—anywhere her scent might linger. Her heart pounded as she reached the rushing river. She crouched, gulping the cold water in greedy, desperate swallows. The chill ran through her, but there was no time to savor the relief. The barks grew louder. Closer. Forcing herself to move, she staggered to her feet and ran again, her legs screaming with exhaustion. The open fields stretched before her, but she knew—no matter how fast she ran, she couldn't outrun the hounds forever. Her chest ached, every breath sharp and shallow. She couldn't keep this pace. She needed air. She needed time. But time had run out.

"I see you, nigger!" the voices shouted from close behind. "Come here, nigger! Stop running!"

She forced one foot in front of the other, clutching her swollen stomach. Every step was agony, her breath ragged, her strength fading. The burden of new life inside her slowed her down, each movement a battle against her own failing body.

"Gotcha, nigger!" The voices rang out over the thunder of galloping hooves and the snarls of hunting dogs.

A sharp jerk wrenched her backward—the rope tightened around her neck, stealing what little air she had left. She collapsed, her hands clawing at the noose as she gasped for breath.

"You thought your black ass could get away from us?"

"Not today, not tomorrow, not ever, you black bitch!"

The white man on horseback yanked the rope, dragging her nearly a mile back to the plantation, where the master stood waiting. The coarse red clay burned against her raw skin as she was pulled across the scorching southern ground. Dust clung to her sweat-soaked body; her fingers still pressed protectively against her stomach even as her strength drained away.

By the time they reached the plantation, the skin on her back had begun to blister from the heat and the brutal dragging. Sweat poured from every pore as the rope was slung over the thick branch of a tree.

"I told your black ass you were mine," the master whispered in her ear. "You black bitch."

"I been watching you for a while now, you and that other nigger slave."

"That baby inside your stomach ain't mine."

"You think you was gonna run off and marry him?" The plantation master rose from his chair, his expression unreadable, and motioned for his overseers to proceed with his previous orders. Not far from the lynching tree, the voice of a pastor echoed through the thick air. "I am the God of Abraham, the God of Isaac, and the God of Jacob," he declared. "God is not the God of the dead, but of the living." The heavy Alabama air clung to the skin, thick with the stench of sweat, soil, and something far worse—fear. Beneath the twisted, gnarled branches of the lynching tree, a gathering of black faces sat in silent observation. They were dressed in their finest clothes, some gifted by their masters, others stitched together with trembling hands. Though their bodies remained still, their souls felt tethered, bound to the horror unfolding before them. They heard the overseers speak, but their eyes—dark, hollow, unwilling to look away—were locked on the body hanging in the stifling heat. The woman, limp and lifeless, swayed slightly, her feet just inches from the earth, the thick rope biting into the flesh of her throat. The tree held her up as if even the ground refused to welcome her back.

The onlookers—helpless, bound by a terror deeper than any chain—sat in silence as their sister swung in the humid, suffocating air. Their powerlessness clung to them like a shroud, an iron grip that shackled not just their bodies but their very souls.

Her suffering was their suffering. Her death, their death.

Her breath had become shallow, each labored inhale a desperate reach for life that never came.

As the men below pulled the rope tighter, her feet lifted from the ground, her body convulsing in violent spasms as the last traces of air slipped from her lungs. Every moment dragged her closer to the end, and with each agonizing second, Shekhinah felt it. She felt her sister's pain, her struggle, her terror—as if it were her own. The gasps filled her mind, as if her lungs were collapsing, as if her own body were trembling beneath the noose. Every shudder, every last desperate tremor of the dying woman, sent a cruel echo through Shekhinah's bones. And then—nothing. The body hung still, swaying in the warm Confederate breeze, discarded like a broken thing. But her hands—those hands, bloody and broken—remained clenched around the secret that would never be spoken. The life that had once grown inside her had now been stolen by hands more brutal than any storm.

Nearby, a fire raged—molten and insatiable, fed for hours in preparation. At its core, an iron blade rested, glowing a fiery orange, an instrument of cruelty forged for the master's every twisted, racist command. The blade, like a coiled viper, quivered with anticipation.

The white man approached, his steps slow and measured, eyes gleaming with satisfaction. He reached into the fire, pulling the blade from its searing heat, the metal radiating a sinister hunger. Turning, he lifted the weapon—a mark of his dominance and hatred—and aimed it at the lifeless woman suspended before him.

With calculated malice, he pressed the iron against her flesh, the burning metal branding her lifeless body. It slid downward, carving a deep, brutal path from her chest to her womb.

Shekhinah jolted awake, her body trembling with raw terror, her heart pounding against her ribs. The nightmare's darkness clung to her, thick and suffocating, as fear clawed at her very soul. She gasped for breath, as if the air had been stolen from her lungs. Her mind, still trapped in the vision's grip, reeled with the sickening realization that something far worse than death was unfolding—a horror too monstrous to escape.

Was this the future of her creations? Pain and suffering? Slavery? The questions gnawed at her.

How did this happen? Why didn't King Abu intervene? Why didn't my father stop this?

Shaken by the vision—this harrowing glimpse of despair—Shekhinah's shock quickly turned to fury. And in that moment, she made a decision that would alter the course of mankind forever. "But Grandmother, I've never heard this story before."

"Where did it begin?"

"What does the Elohim have to do with this drum?"

"And what do they have to do with us?" Ibrahim asked.

"Has Pastor Thomas ever heard this before?"

"Fuck Pastor Thomas," Eshe shouted, laughing. "He don't know shit, and neither do you!"

"Oh, grandson, you have so much to learn," Eshe said, her voice tinged with wisdom.

"To know that we know what we know, and that we do not know what we do not know—that is true knowledge," she continued.

"Who said that, Grandmother? And what does it even mean?" Ibrahim asked, his tone dripping with sarcasm.

"That's a quote from Confucius, and it means you think you know something, but you really don't know shit!"

Issabella burst into laughter at her grandmother's bluntness. "That's what you get for thinking you know everything!" she teased, her voice ringing with amusement.

"Both of you, listen closely." Eshe's voice grew urgent, her frail hands gripping theirs with unexpected strength. "This part of the story is the key to everything. The key to your journey."

Ibrahim, his heart pounding, leaned in. "What journey, Grandmother?"

Eshe's gaze locked onto his, piercing and unwavering. "The journey where you decide who you want to be. The journey that will determine the fate of all humankind."

A hush fell over the room. Issabella's breath caught in her throat. "The fate of humankind?" she whispered, as though uttering the words might unravel the very world they knew.

Eshe nodded slowly, her voice thick with meaning. "This story has been passed down through generations in our family. A story that has no ending—not yet. But you, Ibrahim, and you, Issabella—you are the ones who will write its conclusion."

Her eyes shone with a mix of reverence and urgency. "You are the creators of a new vision. A vision that will shape humanity—past, present, and future."

The silence in the room was suffocating. Time itself seemed to pause, the air heavy with the weight of Eshe's words.

"Do you understand what this means?" Eshe asked softly, her strength fading. "The burden of this decision? The power in your hands?"

Issabella squeezed her grandmother's hand, her mind racing with the enormity of the prophecy unfolding before them. Ibrahim stood motionless, the depth of his role sinking in with every heartbeat.

"You are the ones who will write the ending of this story," Eshe whispered, her voice barely more than a breath. "And with that, you will change everything."

With those final words, her eyes drifted closed, leaving a world of possibilities hanging in the air, as though fate itself was waiting for them to decide which path lay ahead.

And so, the journey began.

CHAPTER 4

"OUR FATHER WHO ART IN HEAVEN"

The vision gripped Shekhinah, wrapping her in a suffocating shroud of terror, as though the very essence of her being was unraveling before her. In a dazed stupor, she stumbled through the shifting shadows, drawn toward the enigmatic Kingdom of the Fifth Heaven, her heart pounding with a chilling urgency. She had witnessed horrors beyond words—unspeakable agony, an unrelenting tide of suffering that clawed at her soul.

Only one held the answers she desperately sought: her brother, Gabri'El. His wisdom and foresight were her last hope of making sense of the nightmare that had taken root in her mind.

As she stepped into the gleaming halls, their brilliance a stark contrast to the darkness still clinging to her, Shekhinah's voice shattered the eerie stillness, raw with desperation. "Gabri'El! You must aid me! I've glimpsed something dreadful... darkness unlike any other. What is this nightmare?"

Gabri'El, the steady anchor in her storm, turned to meet her gaze. His once-sharp eyes softened as he sensed the depth of her terror. Wordlessly, he approached, placing his hands gently upon her head, his warmth a stark contrast to the chilling dread seeping through her. As his essence merged with hers, he absorbed the vision—fear and confusion crashing over him in an instant.

What he saw made his heart shudder—a life stolen before birth, a child lost to the void, the cruel chains of bondage, and the slow decay of humanity's very soul. The burden of her vision settled upon him, heavier than the heavens themselves.

The silence between them grew thick, tension crackling like static in the air. At last, Gabri'El spoke, his voice a low whisper that sent chills racing down Shekhinah's spine. "This... this is their future." His words cut through the stillness like a blade.

"The fate of mankind," he murmured, his tone heavy with finality. "Their destiny—a cycle of suffering, betrayal, and despair. Their punishment for straying from the Creator's path."

Her breath caught, his words striking like a dagger. "No... This cannot be. How could they fall so far?"

Yet something in Gabri'El's expression shifted, a shadow flickering behind his sorrow. Shekhinah's voice trembled with disbelief. "You mourn for them?" she asked, her fear and confusion rising like a tide.

Gabri'El's face was lined with sorrow, but his eyes burned with something deeper—an anguish that could not be soothed. "No, Shekhinah," he said, his tone unwavering. "I do not weep for them."

Her heart skipped a beat. "Then for whom, brother? Who do you mourn?"

His hand, once gentle, tightened around her shoulder. "I mourn for you, Shekhinah. I mourn for the creation you cherish. I mourn for the pain they'll suffer, for the destruction they'll bring upon themselves."

A cold shiver rushed through Shekhinah's chest. Imagining her beloved humanity spiraling into ruin twisted her heart. "What is this war you speak of?" she asked, her voice trembling.

Gabri'El's expression darkened, his voice dropping to a low, ominous tone. "It begins with the first humans—Audam and his companion. But they were led astray. Audam fell under Eve's influence, and Eve... she was deceived by the Serpent."

Shekhinah's thoughts spun. "Wait—who is Eve?"

Gabri'El sighed deeply, the sound heavy with sorrow. "While you slept, the world changed. Your first creation, Lilith—the one you shaped from the dust of the earth—grew restless. She defied Audam and allied herself with the Fallen One—the Serpent. And so, in his sorrow, the Creator formed another companion for Audam from his flesh. Her name was Eve."

The revelation struck Shekhinah like thunder. "But... she was deceived as well?" she whispered, her voice shaking with disbelief.

Gabri'El nodded solemnly, his gaze unwavering. "Yes. Both Eve and Audam fell victim to the Serpent's lies. Humanity has wandered lost ever since. They no longer honor the Creator; they've forgotten their true purpose. They're weak, Shekhinah, drifting without direction."

A fierce surge of anger burned within Shekhinah's chest. "Blasphemy!" she cried. "How can this be? Will Ekiku fall as well? Is there nothing we can do to prevent this fate?"

Gabri'El's face darkened, his expression carved with sorrow older than time itself. "Their downfall, Shekhinah, is bound to one of us— one of our own."

Shekhinah's heart quickened. "One of us? How is that possible? How could any of the Elohim betray the Creator and bring ruin upon the earth?"

Gabri'El leaned closer, his voice dropping to a dangerous whisper, heavy with painful truth. "It is our eldest brother. The first, the greatest among us: Lucifer."

The name hit Shekhinah like a strike to her core. "Lucifer? No... He loves the Creator! He loves us! How could he?"

Gabri'El's cold, relentless eyes met hers. "He loves the Creator, yes. But he despises what the Creator has made. He resents that humanity was granted free will—something he, in his arrogance, believes should belong only to him. Lucifer feels betrayed by the Creator, and thus, he's turned against us all. He's turned against the Creator."

Shekhinah struggled to breathe. "Lucifer... he would never betray us."

Gabri'El's expression hardened with determination. "He already has. Lucifer has broken his bond with the Kingdom, and the storm of war approaches. Nothing can stop it now. He has gathered his followers, intending to corrupt humanity and lead them into darkness. War is inevitable."

"No," Shekhinah whispered, shaking her head in disbelief. "Surely... there must be another way."

Gabri'El stood still, the burden of creation pressing upon him. "There is no other way, Shekhinah. War draws near, and humanity's suffering will be a part of it. Lucifer's rebellion has already begun; the path is set."

The fire within Shekhinah burned brighter, strengthening her resolve. "Then I will plead with the Creator. I refuse to stand by helplessly. I will protect humanity—I will not let them fall."

Gabri'El's eyes glistened with sorrow so deep it seemed to echo across the heavens. "You cannot stop this, Shekhinah. Events have been set into motion. Lucifer has chosen his course, and many will follow him."

Shekhinah stood firm, her eyes blazing with fierce determination. "Then I will carve my path. I will fight for humanity. I will appeal directly to the Creator and ensure this story does not end in despair."

For a heartbeat, silence surrounded them, heavy with unavoidable fate. Gabri'El bowed his head, burdened by the harsh truth. "If you must, sister. But there is no turning back now. The war has already begun."

With that, Shekhinah turned, her heart burning with defiance. She would approach the Creator; she would battle for the fate of all she had shaped. The struggle for humanity's soul had only just begun.

"Grandmother, why did the Creator allow us to fail?"

Her gaze drifted far away, as if looking beyond the curtain of time itself. The silence grew, thick and intense, before she finally spoke, her voice soft and filled with hidden truths.

"Do not trouble yourself with such questions," she whispered. "All will become clear as the story unfolds. But heed my words—forget everything you believe you know. The stories they've told you are lies, carefully constructed to conceal a darker truth—a truth yet to be revealed."

Her eyes grew dark as she spoke, as though the universe itself held its breath.

CHAPTER 5

"FATHER, WHY HAVE YOU FORSAKEN ME?"

Shekhinah ascended to the Tenth Heaven, the highest realm, determined to seek her Father's mercy for humanity's survival. The fate of her creation pressed heavily upon her heart. She knew it would not be simple, for her plea would ignite great conflict with the Creator. Yet her resolve remained firm. Her mind raced with troubling thoughts: What if the Creator rejects my plea? What if He denies my request to save humanity? The thought brought deep anguish. If He refused, all her efforts would crumble. But Shekhinah pressed onward, undaunted. She would never surrender.

If anyone could save humanity, it was her, and she believed only her Father possessed the wisdom and power needed.

Two days of tireless travel through the highest realms brought Shekhinah to the Creator's dwelling. She approached the great chamber, her heart burdened by hope and fear, and knocked three times upon the door. Silence lingered, heavy and oppressive. She knocked again, three sharp strikes. A powerful voice echoed from within, filled equally with authority and displeasure: "Who dares disturb me?" "It is I, Father," Shekhinah replied, her voice trembling yet resolute. "Your most faithful servant, Shekhinah."

The voice softened slightly but remained firm: "And why have you come, Daughter?"

With tears pooling in her eyes, Shekhinah replied, "Father, I come to beg your mercy. Our creation, humanity, suffers greatly. They're blind to the future awaiting them—a future filled with pain, despair, and darkness. I ask, Father, for your wisdom and strength to guide them. Allow me to intervene on their behalf. Let me bring them peace."

A long, uneasy silence filled the chamber before the Creator responded, "And what has humanity done to deserve my favor, Shekhinah? How have they earned my grace?"

Shekhinah's heart filled with profound, aching love for humanity. "Father, they have praised You with all their strength, though they understand so little of You. From what little we gave them, they've created much. They haven't forgotten Your name or Your deeds. For generations, they've honored You. They love You in every way they know how, Father."

The Creator's voice grew colder. "Yet, Daughter, ever since I granted them knowledge and intellect, they've turned against one another. They've spilled their blood. They've filled the earth with violence, power struggles, and warfare. Brothers kill brothers, sons rise against their fathers, and nations battle one another. They chose darkness when I offered them a choice—the blessing of My light, or temptation in shadow. They embraced darkness. And now you plead for their forgiveness?"

Shekhinah's voice broke with desperation. "Yes, Father. I plead forgiveness for them. Allow me to return to them. Let me reveal a new path. Let me guide them toward redemption. I know they've chosen darkness, yet I still believe in them. I believe they can return to the light."

The Creator's voice softened but remained firm. "I understand your compassion for them, Daughter. But humanity has made its choice. The path they walk is of their choosing. Their suffering results from their actions. I will not undo what has begun."

Shekhinah's heart shattered. She sank to her knees, her Father's words crushing her spirit. "Father, why do you abandon me? They've done nothing wrong but worship You. Yes, they're lost, but they've never forsaken You. Must they suffer for their mistakes? I can't stand aside and watch them descend into pain and violence. Please, Father, let me help them."

Harshness edged the Creator's voice now. "You will not aid them, Shekhinah. If you defy Me—if you disobey My command—you will be cast from this realm. You will no longer belong to this Kingdom."

Shekhinah bowed her head, grief pressing upon her heart. Her pleas had gone unheard. The Creator had spoken. There would be no mercy. As Gabri'El predicted, her Father remained silent, unmoved. Yet the path forward became clear to Shekhinah: if no one else intervened, she would. She felt alone in her plight to save humanity.

Shekhinah knew that without her action, humankind would soon face the greatest cruelty imaginable—slavery, centuries of torment, and an unbreakable bond with Lucifer. She was their Creator, and if anyone could change their destiny, it was her.

But she also knew that this act would come at a great cost. To save them, she would have to leave Heaven. She would have to forsake her place among the Elohim and live as a mortal, among the very beings she had created. It would be a sacrifice of her birthright—a sacrifice she was willing to make for the sake of the people she had fashioned with her own hands.

Before she left, Shekhinah sought out her brother, Gabri'El, with a final request. She was the only one, besides the Creator, who knew that Gabri'El possessed the serpent's skin—the skin of the original Serpent of Eden. Whoever held it had the power to control the ripples of time itself. Shekhinah planned to leave Heaven and journey to Earth, but she needed the serpent's skin to ensure that she arrived at the right time.

She approached Gabri'El's quarters quietly, hoping to retrieve the skin without his knowledge or consent. She searched through his chambers, but it was not there. After a long moment of contemplation, Shekhinah realized where Gabri'El would hide it—among the beauties of Earth, hidden in plain sight. The serpent's skin had to be hidden in the very heart of the Earth itself, where no one other than Elohim would have knowledge of looking.

Her journey would take her to a hidden pyramid, deep within a lush forest near the western coast of Africa. This pyramid, visible from the Heavens but hidden to those on Earth, was where the Creator had hidden the Tree of Knowledge once it was cast out of Eden. Shekhinah knew this place well—it was the very location where she had created the first humans, Audum and Lilith.

But Shekhinah knew that her journey would come with immense consequences. If she left Heaven; it would be her last time in her Elohim form. She would be sacrificing her divine status to live among mortals, to become one of them, and to guide them back to the light.

With a heavy heart but a clear resolve, Shekhinah transformed herself into a bolt of lightning and descended to Earth, her essence crackling with energy. When she landed, her form lay flat against the ground, and the smoke that rose from her body signified her transformation. She looked down at herself, amazed to see that she now bore the same anatomy as her first female creation, Lilith, from millennia ago. The gravity of the Earth was unfamiliar, but Shekhinah quickly adjusted, feeling her senses sharpen.

As she stood and began her journey toward the pyramid, a powerful sense of destiny surged within her. She was here to save humanity, regardless of the price. And so, Shekhinah walked into the unknown, leaving her divine birthright behind, determined to rewrite the fate of humanity. Her senses of sight and sound quickly adjusted to her new environment after she slowed her breathing. The freshness of the night air and the wet ground stimulated the pores of her skin and nose. As she was now in complete control of her bodily senses, she walked to a small clearing.

Shekhinah stepped into the unknown, leaving behind her divine heritage, determined to rewrite humanity's future. After slowing her breathing, her vision and hearing quickly adjusted to her new surroundings. The coolness of the night air and the damp earth stimulated her skin and sense of smell. Now fully in command of her human senses, she moved toward a small clearing, realizing she'd landed atop the hidden pyramid. "I am here," she whispered. She gazed upward at the enormous tree before her, nearly thirty-three feet tall, its leaves shimmering beneath the starlit sky.

Twelve feet ahead lay the reflective pool, which had revealed her image moments earlier. It stood as the sole barrier between Shekhinah and the glistening green skin wrapped around the massive trunk of the Tree of Knowledge.

As Shekhinah walked across the large body of water toward the tree, each step stirred the water, causing creatures to rise to the surface as if drawn to her presence. As she neared the Tree of Knowledge, a strange energy filled the air—her arm hairs stood on end, and even the bark's fine bristles seemed to respond, as though the tree itself recognized her arrival and purpose.

With the serpent's skin now tightly wrapped around her right arm, she descended the pyramid steps into a small clearing among the trees. The rustling of night creatures faded as she entered, their hurried retreat confirming what her senses had already told her—she was not alone.

On this misty African night, a young man stood hidden behind a tree, watching her every move. A tense silence stretched between them.

Then, cautiously, he stepped forward, spear raised above his head, ready to strike at the first sign of danger.

Shekhinah, now fully on guard but possessing no special powers, stepped into the moonlight, her completely bare form revealed beneath the glow. Her long, flowing red hair cascaded down her back, framing her figure. The moonlight traced every curve of her body, casting deep shadows and soft highlights across her dark chocolate skin, which shimmered under the night sky. Everything about her presence exuded divinity.

The young man froze at the sight of her, his breath catching in his throat. A rush of heat surged through him as he took in the fullness of her form—every contour, every detail that marked her as a woman. The tension in his grip loosened, and his spear slowly lowered to his side. Any thought of danger vanished, replaced by a sense of reverence and overwhelming attraction. He, too, wore only a simple covering of fig leaves around his waist, now unsettled by the undeniable response of his body to the woman standing before him. Embarrassed, he instinctively reached for himself, trying to conceal the evidence of his desire. Shekhinah stepped closer, her presence nearly overwhelming.

With an unsteady breath, the young man removed a single fig leaf from his covering and gently placed it over Shekhinah's womanhood, shielding her from his own tempted gaze. Then, in a voice both soft and resolute, he asked,

"Are you part of my rites of passage to become a man?"

"Did my father place you here to surprise me?"

"I am Prince Obatala, the heir to the crown. Who are you?"

Issabella leaned in, her voice barely above a whisper. "So, Grandmother... was this Shekhinah a fallen angel?" The old woman's eyes darkened, the firelight casting eerie shadows across her weathered face. She hesitated before speaking, her voice low, almost conspiratorial.

"The original one, baby girl," she said slowly, stretching each word as if unraveling a long-buried secret. "She was the first to descend from heaven... in an attempt to save mankind from his sins." Issabella's breath hitched, but before she could respond, Ishmael interjected, his tone edged with doubt.

"But we were taught that Lucifer was the first fallen angel. That he and his followers rebelled, waging war against God..." His voice faded, uncertainty creeping in. The grandmother's gaze locked onto him, her eyes unyielding. "No, my son," she said, each syllable weighed with meaning. "Shekhinah wanted to alter time itself. She sought to undo the betrayal... the one committed by the serpent." Her words hung in the air, thick with unspoken danger. Ishmael and Issabella exchanged uneasy glances, the weight of her revelation pressing down on them like an impending storm. But the grandmother was not finished. She leaned forward, her eyes gleaming with an intensity that sent chills through the room.

"But don't worry," she continued, her voice barely above a whisper. "All will become clear as the story unfolds. But I need you to forget everything you thought you knew... because everything—every single thing—has been a lie. A carefully constructed deception designed to shape a dark narrative, one that has yet to be fully revealed." The air grew heavy with tension, the silence that followed nearly suffocating. It felt as though the very walls were closing in, as if something ancient and forbidden was about to surface—an unsettling truth so immense, so powerful, that once uncovered, it could never be undone.

CHAPTER 6

"BIRTH OF ROYAL BLOOD"

The searing pain coursing through her body paralyzed her thoughts as she staggered through the door of the peaceful sanctuary. The Queen gasped for water, her mouth dry from the sudden, unbearable agony overtaking her. Just moments ago, she had been resting comfortably, unaware of the storm brewing within her.

Now, with each relentless squeeze and release of her womb, she cried out as if it were her last breath. Her screams tore through the royal birthing chambers, carrying across the nearby forest, rousing every creature from its slumber.

Sweat drenched her forehead, streaming down her trembling body as waves of heat and chills coursed through her. Her muscles quaked in torment, her strength waning under the relentless grip of labor. Her three midwives hovered close, their hands steady but their eyes filled with urgency, whispering words of comfort as the contractions came faster and stronger, unlike anything she had ever known.

"Is this normal? Am I dying?" the queen asked, her voice strained with fear.

Queen Anumatra was in labor for the first time in her life. Every previous pregnancy had ended in a sudden, heartbreaking miscarriage. Yet, those painful losses were not in vain—they had led her to this very moment, a moment of hope and triumph. This child was a gift from the Orishas, destined to survive.

This labor was more than just the act of childbirth; it was the fulfillment of her deepest prayers. It was not only the birth of an heir but the pinnacle of her womanhood. She understood its significance, much like the blossoms of spring that promised fruit to nourish her kingdom. This child was not just her future—it was the kingdom's future, a beacon of hope and renewal.

As she stood on the birthing blocks, her midwives steadied her fragile frame, keeping her upright as each contraction wracked her body with unbearable pain. Her mother's soothing words washed over her, a lifeline amid the storm. Between the crushing waves of labor, she stole brief moments to collect herself, taking slow sips of cold water before the next wave of agony seized her once more.

Queen Anumatra and King Obattalla had been married for thirteen years, yet there had never been the slightest prospect of a successful pregnancy that would bless them with a child. For years, she had prayed to the ancestors, offered countless sacrifices to the Orishas, and wept for the heir her husband longed for. She had feared her prayers had gone unanswered—until now.

Her mother, Naomi, sat beside her, stroking her long, thick curls with steady hands. She moved with practiced ease, massaging away the tension between her fingers and along her trembling arms. Beads of sweat clung to Queen Anumatra's deep, radiant skin, glistening under the sharp moonlight streaming through the birthing chamber's open roof.

Naomi's voice never wavered, her whispered prayers rising steadily, an offering of gratitude to the ancestors and the heavenly Orishas. "It is almost time," she murmured.

The Queen's breath quickened—equal parts excitement and fear—her body coiled in anticipation of the moment she had longed for. "Push, my Queen," the midwives urged, their voices urgent yet steady.

Naomi's grip tightened as Anumatra's cries pierced the night. "Push harder, Queen! Breathe! In and out!"

Then, just as relief crept in, she glanced down and saw it—the crown of her baby's head easing into the crisp night air.

"Agggggggg!!!!" The Queen's scream ripped through the chamber as she gave one final, desperate push.

And then, with one last surge of breath, a thrust of her hips, and the collective prayers of all present, Queen Anumatra brought forth new life. The baby slipped into the waiting hands of the midwives, the warm embrace of Naomi, and the boundless love of a mother who had waited a lifetime for this moment.

Meanwhile, just outside the birthing quarters, King Obatala paced back and forth, his steps quickening in rhythm with his racing heartbeat. His mind was a storm of fear and relief—two opposing forces clashing within him as he realized the moment he had impatiently awaited for the past nine months was finally here. A chill ran through him, as if ice water coursed through his veins. His mouth went dry, his stomach twisted with the weight of uncertainty.

Above, the heavens rumbled with flashes of lightning and the thunderous voices of the Gods speaking to their creation below. A steady rain drummed against the forest leaves, softening the earth beneath his bare feet until they pressed into the nutrient-rich soil of the village.

King Obatala had waited for this precise moment in time—the very moment foretold to him by the tribal medicine woman over three years ago. She had prophesied that his heir would take their first breath on a cool, rain-kissed night such as this. She had spoken of a child destined to lead their people across vast oceans, to endure great despair, trials, and tribulations, but ultimately, to bring peace and redemption to their land.

Though excitement swelled within him, his pulse thundered in anticipation. Anticipation of the life he had created, just as his ancestors had created him. Anticipation of the moment, thirteen years from now, when he would pass down the crown—just as it had been passed down through generations before him.

Obatala, fully aware of his nervousness, walked down to the ocean, hoping to steady his thoughts. He wanted to remain close, just in case the drums announced that the time had come. His steps carried him only a short distance from the birthing quarters, no farther than a brief sprint away from the dwelling where his queen had labored for days.

The moment his feet touched the beach, a wave of solace washed over him. The rhythmic crash of the ocean against the shore filled his ears, drowning out the turmoil within. The cool, misty breeze settled over his dark, glistening skin, seeping into his pores and easing the tension from his body. His pulse slowed, his restless thoughts untangling into words he could finally give voice to.

Standing firm against the ocean's embrace, Obatala felt his body sync with the water's rhythm, as if he had become part of the symphony of waves. The pounding in his chest faded. His breath no longer came in shallow gasps but deep, steady draws of cool, salt-tinged air. The queasiness from the celebratory feast earlier that night melted away.

He and the ocean were now one—one beat, one rhythm, one song, rising in harmony with the heavens and the ancestors in gratitude for this sacred night.

This was the night when the constellation Capricorn positioned itself in the northern hemisphere, beginning its journey across the vast African sky. The Winter Solstice was one of the most sacred days on the Ebonee Tribal solar calendar—a night thick with anticipation, for it marked a celestial turning point.

By dawn, the sun would appear eerily still upon the horizon, frozen in place, unmoving. Its pause would cast an unsettling presence over the land. But on the third day... the third day would bring renewal. The sun would begin its slow ascent, creeping northward by a single degree each day until it reached its final reckoning on the Spring Equinox. The world would hold its breath, watching and waiting as the sun's return signified the unfolding of something far greater.

To the Ebonee people, the constellation Capricorn carried a long and storied past. Since his earliest memories, King Obatala had known his people as sailors and explorers, venturing far beyond the lands of their ancestors. They not only traveled by foot, uncovering the vast beauty of Africa, but they also braved the seas, navigating their way to distant western continents.

The oral histories passed down to him from his father and grandfather remained etched in his mind. He had listened intently as they recounted tales of voyages across the vast ocean, of encounters with foreign lands, traders, and hunters from regions above and below the equatorial line. These stories were more than memories; they were testaments to the resilience and boundless spirit of his people.

His kingdom flourished with fields of tobacco and corn—crops not native to his homeland but to lands far west across the Atlantic Ocean. Spices once found only in the distant East now thrived within the walls of the Ebonee kingdom. These were the rewards of trade and travel, a testament to his people's connection with distant nations.

In addition to being skilled traders, his people were master shipbuilders and expert sailors. Their craftsmanship was so revered that neighboring nations sought their ships, granting them political influence and strategic alliances. Through generations of skillful trade and diplomacy, his great kingdom had amassed unparalleled wealth and power. Through this legacy of success, King Obatala rose to become the richest and wisest of all kings across the vast continent of Africa.

Now, he stood as a proud ruler, awaiting his heir, ready to embrace whatever the night would bring. Obatala's mind drifted back to his childhood, to the days when he roamed freely in the innocence of boyhood. He recalled the trials that had shaped him into a man—the sacred rites, the lessons of endurance, and the wisdom passed down by the elders. Those seven nights alone in the forest had left him with questions that time had only begun to answer. But now, his mind was at ease. His pulse was steady. He listened, waiting for the sound of the drums to summon him—to call him forward to greet his seed.

As he stood by the ocean, lost in his thoughts, the rain ceased, and the heavens parted, allowing the full moon to cast its brilliance upon the clear, starry African sky. His breaths were long and steady, his heart at peace. For a brief moment, all was still.

But his tranquility was shattered by the hurried footsteps of his most trusted and loyal general, Shango.

"Great King, I bring you the update you requested."

"Speak freely, General," Obatala replied, his voice low, laced with anticipation.

Shango bowed slightly before delivering the news. "My King, you have a daughter, and your concubine requests your presence at once. She is not well."

Before Obatala could respond, the ceremonial drums thundered through the night, their echo carrying across the kingdom. Moments later, the sound of a newborn's cry followed, weaving into the rhythm of celebration. The people rejoiced, their voices rising in praise, their feet moving in joyous dance. Before sprinting toward the sound of the drums, Obatala dropped to his knees, bowing his head in gratitude. He whispered his thanks to the great Orishas for the gift of his seed, his firstborn. But as the weight of his joy settled, so too did the burden of his guilt.

He would not only ask for blessings, but also ask for forgiveness. Forgiveness for his sins, his transgressions, and the choices he had made as a king, choices that would not be looked upon favorably by his ancestors or his people.

He knew this night, like all nights, carried its omens. The drums did not simply announce birth; they announced revelation.

Just as the clouds had parted to reveal the moonlight, the truth, too, would be unveiled. And he would have to face it.

A secret known only to him and the dark recesses of his subconscious. A secret both strange and unnatural—yet divine in its origin. A secret that had taken on a life of its own, its mere existence threatening to crumble the very foundation of his kingdom. But it was more than that.

This secret not only endangered his rule; it threatened to unravel everything he understood about science, humanity, and the order of the world itself. It was a secret that had followed him from childhood to the height of his reign. A secret he had first witnessed as a boy—falling from the heavens, descending from the stars. "But Grandmother, who was the little girl that was born?" Issabella's voice trembled, caught between curiosity and unease. "And why is it so important that she was born first?" Eshe's gaze darkened, her eyes reflecting knowledge too dangerous to be spoken aloud.

"The king had a secret daughter," she said, her voice slow and deliberate, as if each word carried the burden of centuries. Issabella's heart pounded. "What?" she whispered, the air around her growing thick with mystery. Before she could say another word, Eshe pressed on, her tone weighted with the gravity of ancient truths.

"Well, granddaughter, her name was Ayisha," Eshe continued, her voice barely more than a whisper. "She was the daughter of Shekhinah, and her father was the King. And on that fateful night, when the moon was hidden behind dark clouds, the Queen gave birth to a son—Ogunwale."

Issabella's mind spun, struggling to grasp the weight of Eshe's words. But before she could fully process them, Ishmael, unable to contain his disbelief, cut in.

"Grandmother… she was his sister?" he asked, his voice thick with shock. "So… they were brother and sister?" Eshe nodded slowly, her eyes glinting with an eerie, knowing light.

"Yes, they were. Twins, though not from the same womb. Born on the same day, in the same year, just three minutes apart. Twins, like you two, but not of the same bloodline. Not of the same mother."

A thick silence fell over the room, pressing against them like an unseen force. It was as if the very walls had paused, waiting for the weight of this revelation to settle.

Issabella's pulse thundered in her ears. Twins? Brother and sister? The secrets were unraveling faster than she could make sense of them. But Ishmael wasn't finished.

"Well, Grandmother," he pressed, urgency laced in his voice. "Who was to rule the nation? I thought in royal lineages, the firstborn had the right to the throne?"

Eshe's expression gentled, though it offered no comfort. She nodded slowly. "Yes, grandson," she replied softly, her voice barely above a whisper. "That is what the law commands."

"But how can this be?" Ishmael's voice cracked with frustration. "How can she be the firstborn and yet—"

"Grandmother, if that's true…it's adding insult to injury!" Ishmael interrupted, anger flaring.

"Exactly," Eshe's voice grew solemn, her words burdened with centuries of sorrow. "In those days, women were highly honored, especially within royal bloodlines. However, a woman ascending the throne, particularly one born under secretive and forbidden circumstances, would have thrown all of Africa into chaos. "Obatala's secret was no mere family matter; it was a force veiled in ancient silence, potent enough to unhinge the balance of realms, not only in Africa, but across the very fabric of the world itself."

Her words lingered in the room, heavy like the quiet before a storm. As silence settled, the air grew colder, darker. Eshe's breath became shallow, as though the burden of truth pressed upon her, sapping her strength.

"Now," Eshe's voice trembled, but carried the authority of generations. "The time has come for the bloodline to be restored. The secret—the one concealed in shadows, hidden within layers of time—a secret so powerful, so dangerous, that it has driven men and women alike to commit unspeakable acts…must finally be exposed. It can no longer remain buried in the dark corners of forgotten places. The moment is here. Truths shrouded in mystery must emerge, for they hold the key to boundless power and consequences beyond imagination."

As the world unknowingly balanced on the brink of discovery, the price of this knowledge—capable of unraveling everything—would be paid in blood. The secret, once spoken only in fear, now demanded revelation.

Eshe's breathing grew increasingly strained, and Ishmael and Issabella felt the ground beneath them shift. The story they believed they knew began to collapse before their eyes, replaced by something darker, more perilous, and infinitely more intricate.

The fire hissed ominously, but Eshe's eyes were distant, as if witnessing something beyond their sight.

"Listen carefully, my dears," she whispered, voice shaking. "Pay close attention, for what comes next…will change everything."

In her words, the shadows seemed to tighten around them, as though the room itself held its breath, awaiting the truth—and the inevitable transformation of the world.

CHAPTER 7

"A KING'S' DECEIT"

As the years passed, King Obatala, ruler of the Ebonee Kingdom, found himself consumed by an insidious regret—one that gnawed at his mind, darkening his every thought. His reign had brought prosperity to the kingdom, and his people had thrived, yet the burden of his hidden sins cast an ever-present shadow. He knew the truth could never be revealed, for if it were, both he and the daughter he kept locked away would meet a brutal end, their blood soaking the soil of Ebonee.

The victories that once filled him with pride, the conquests that had strengthened Ebonee's rule, now felt hollow, tainted by the choices he had made. General Shango, once a hero in the eyes of the people, had fallen by Obatala's hand—a necessary act at the time, yet one that refused to fade from his conscience. The memory of Shango's death clung to him like a curse, a wound that would never close.

Still, the king knew he could not dwell on the past. New threats loomed, fresh battles awaited, and the kingdom's survival demanded his focus. So, he buried his regrets deep, forcing himself to look ahead and protect the realm he had built.

Two decades had passed since the assassination of General Shango, and now an aging Obatala prepared to pass the throne to his son, Ogunwale. The young prince had already proven himself as a formidable leader, guiding the kingdom to victory in the grueling seven-day war against the Europeans. Yet, beneath his triumph, an unseen danger lurked—one that threatened to undo everything. The Europeans, driven by an insatiable thirst for power, had set their sights on the Ebonee, drawn to its fertile lands, abundant wealth, and the advanced knowledge Obatala had fiercely protected.

For years, the Europeans had swept through neighboring kingdoms with little resistance. Still, they knew Ebonee would not fall so easily. Instead of launching a direct assault, they devised a calculated scheme—gifting the king and his son advanced weaponry and technology, hoping to lure them into submission. But Obatala, too proud to yield, scoffed at their offerings, knowing his kingdom's innovations far surpassed anything they could provide. Their expressions darkened with anger as they departed, and an unsettling certainty settled in Obatala's mind. They would return—and this time, they would bring war.

When the inevitable battle erupted, it was swift and merciless. For six days, Ebonee's warriors held their ground, their defenses unyielding against wave after wave of foreign invaders. On the seventh day, the tide turned. The Europeans, battered and broken, were driven out, their armies left in disarray. Victorious, the people of Ebonee rejoiced, hailing Obatala and Ogunwale as champions, although it was inevitable that Obatala's time was coming to a close. They pleaded with the king to remain on the throne, to continue leading them through the storm that had yet to pass.

But in the aftermath of victory, Ogunwale, drained and battered from battle, withdrew to his quarters to recover. As he lay on his bed, gazing up at the night sky, the stars seemed distant and indifferent. A fleeting sense of peace settled over him, only to be shattered by a sudden unease. Something was near. Something was waiting.

His pulse quickened as he pushed himself upright, his hand instinctively closing around the hilt of his sword. Outside his chamber, the shadows shifted, and a chill crept through the air. His mind raced. Had the Europeans returned for vengeance? Or had assassins been sent to end his life? Ogunwale quickly opened his eyes and turned his head to scan the room. His observations brought him instant fear as he saw shadows moving outside near the front and rear entrances of his royal quarters. He slowly stood up and drew his sword and dagger in preparation for the battle of his life.

Had the Europeans sought revenge for their defeat?

Had they sent assassins to kill him? Ogunwale was now confused as the shadows had not revealed themselves. His heart raced with uncertainty and fear. His hands were now sweaty and clammy as he anxiously waited for the intruders to reveal themselves.

"Who goes there?" he called, his voice steady despite the surge of adrenaline coursing through him.

A figure stepped into the dim light, and his breath caught in his throat—it was his father, King Obatala. His expression was unreadable, his grip firm around a drawn blade. Before Ogunwale could react, another presence emerged from the darkness, pressing so close that he felt the icy whisper of breath against his skin. Then came the pain—sharp, deep, and merciless. A dagger tore into his back, sending agony ripping through him.

But it was the sight of his father's raised blade, poised above his throat, that broke him.

"It's for the best, my son," Obatala whispered, his voice distant, hollow with finality. "Now go meet your ancestors."

The blade sliced through Ogunwale's throat, and in an instant, his world shattered. Blood gushed from the wound, pooling beneath him as darkness closed in. In those final moments, a sudden light—brilliant, piercing—flooded the room. A woman appeared, her presence both soothing and heavy with warning.

"Resist the darkness in your heart," she murmured, her voice an eerie echo in the growing void. "For the darkness is the great deception of mankind."

His vision blurred, the light fading, and then—nothing.

Ogunwale jolted awake with a sharp breath, alone in his quarters. No shadows. No assassins. His father had not betrayed him. It had been a dream—a harrowing premonition. Yet the fear clung to him, an invisible force pressing against his chest, refusing to let go. Something was wrong. Something was coming. Something far worse than the war they had just survived.

CHAPTER 8

"WHISPERS FROM THE DEPTHS OF DARKNESS"

This dream had left a feeling of fear, confusion, and a horrifying death. These fears were flowing throughout every artery, every vein, and every cell within his being." What did all this mean?" he asked himself.

Frightened, worried, and confused from the visions, he sought out the wisdom of the village medicine woman who lived deep into the woods, far from the village. He knew he needed to understand the whole meaning of this premonition; he needed to seek the assistance of village medicine. Obatala gathered his horse and his weapon and, frantically, left the village confines for the wood where the medicine woman dwelt.

Ogunwale, seeking wisdom and clarity, arrived at the old woman's secluded home, its crooked silhouette looming like a dark secret against the suffocating blackness of the forest. The door seemed to open slowly by itself, as there were no visible door handles. The sun had set completely outside, and darkness was now over the kingdom, and all the forest was even darker. There was no light inside the medicine woman's quarters except for a single candle flickering in the very back room of the small, creepy house.

The air was thick with silence, broken only by the rustling of unseen creatures. This was no ordinary visit—something felt wrong, as if the very ground beneath him carried a warning. He had come here countless times before, but tonight, the shadows seemed to stretch longer, and the house appeared more forbidding.

A dim light seeped through the windows, casting eerie shapes that shifted with the wind. As he stepped closer, the weight of the night bore down on him, dense and unyielding. He knocked three times, each rap slicing through the stillness like a whispered omen. The door creaked open on its own, as though it had been expecting him. Inside, the air was thick with the scent of herbs and something more unsettling. A single candle burned weakly, its glow unsteady, throwing restless shadows across the walls.

"Welcome, Prince Ogunwale," a raspy voice drifted from the dim corner. The old woman sat there, her eyes gleaming unnaturally bright in the darkness, as if she could see straight through him. "I know why you're here."

Ogunwale froze. His pulse pounded, and a cold sweat gathered at his brow. He hadn't spoken a word, yet she already knew. "Do you?" he asked, his voice unsteady. "Yes," she murmured, her slow, knowing smile sending a chill down his spine. "I have watched you since the day you were born. I know who you are... and why you've come." Her words settled over him like a smothering fog. She gestured to a worn chair beside the low-burning fire, its feverish glow deepening the shadows in the room. The flames crackled with a strange, hollow sound, as if something inside them was stirring, watching.

She poured tea into a chipped iron cup and extended it toward him. Her hands trembled—not from age, but from something else, something unseen. "Sit, Prince. Let me help you interpret the meaning of your dream. But first, I must warn you—the truth I offer comes at a price. It is a burden you may not be ready to carry. Once you know, you cannot un-know." Ogunwale hesitated, his thoughts churning. He had come seeking answers, but now a primal fear gnawed at the edges of his mind. The weight of fate hung heavy in the air, and deep inside, he was beginning to understand the truth of her words. But there was no turning back.

"Proceed," he said, his voice barely above a whisper.

The old woman's eyes seemed to deepen, her voice lowering to a rasping whisper. "Your birth, Prince Ogunwale, was no ordinary event. It was a carefully guarded secret, bound to mysteries that stretch far beyond your understanding. Your father, King Obatala, is not who you think he is. The death of General Shango, your mother's strange disappearance—these were no accidents. They were planned. And the dream that haunts you? It is not a warning, but a calling."

Ogunwale's throat tightened. "A calling to what?" he asked, his voice barely audible.

She leaned forward, her face unsettlingly close, and in her eyes burned a cold intensity that chilled his soul. "You have a sister, Prince, born three minutes before you—a daughter of Obatala, hidden in secrecy for years. Her existence... her very blood... holds the rightful claim to the throne." The room seemed to tilt, the walls pressing in. The words struck like a blow to his chest, and for a moment, he couldn't breathe. A sister? Hidden? His mind reeled, struggling to grasp the enormity of it.

"Your father feared her," the old woman continued, her voice now barely a whisper, as if the air itself were listening. "He feared what her existence would mean for his rule, so he buried her, erased her from history. But blood cannot be erased, Prince Ogunwale. And now, the time has come for the truth to surface."

The candle wavered violently, casting grotesque shadows across her face. For the first time, Ogunwale noticed the markings carved into her skin—symbols he had only seen in nightmares. The air grew cold, unnaturally so, and a deep chill settled into his bones—something ancient, something terrible, stirred in the darkness.

"Now that you know," she whispered, her voice a haunting lullaby of doom, "you must decide. Will you seek her out? Will you tear down the lies your father has built, knowing the price you must pay? Or will you leave the past buried and let the shadows consume everything?"

Ogunwale felt the force of her gaze press into him, a dark presence clawing at his soul. The room spun, the walls tightening around him, and he understood—there would be no turning back. No matter his choice, the nightmare had already begun.

"Who is this sister?" Ogunwale asked, his voice barely above a whisper.

"The woman in your dream," the medicine woman said, her tone unwavering. "She is the one who will take the throne if you do not act."

Ogunwale's mind spun. "But I am the heir to the throne! I am King Obatala's only child!"

Ogunwale, still frozen in disbelief, now witnessed the ground beneath him feeling unsteady. His thoughts crashed into one another, confusion swiftly giving way to anger.

"Who is she?" he demanded. "Who is this child who threatens everything I've fought for?"

The medicine woman hesitated; her silence thick with unspoken truth. Then, with a quiet finality, she spoke.

"The girl you love—the one you have been seeing for the past three moons," she said softly, "is your sister. Aiysha."

The words struck Ogunwale like a bolt of lightning. His chest tightened, and the world around him seemed to collapse. "No... that's impossible!" he choked, stumbling backward, as if the force of the revelation had physically hit him.

"Your father," the medicine woman continued, "and Aiysha's mother swore a blood oath to keep her identity hidden, to protect the throne until the time came for her to claim it."

Ogunwale left the medicine woman's home in a daze, his mind spiraling with the cruel truths that had shaped his life. Betrayed by his father, shattered by the revelation of his sister's identity, he knew he could not stand idle.

He would act—not only to secure his place on the throne but to unearth the deeper, darker secrets buried beneath years of deception. He would become the most powerful king in Africa, and he would expose the lies that had long ruled his kingdom.

CHAPTER 9

"QUEEN AYISHA"

For the past three moons, Ayisha and Ogunwale had been in courtship. Their union had been blessed not only by the village elders but also by the elders from the four surrounding kingdoms. King Obatala, Ogunwale's father, had also given his blessing, speaking of a vision in which the ancestors, stretching back five generations, came to him, offering their guidance and approval. The ancestors foretold that Ogunwale and Ayisha's union would be so powerful that it would bring significant change to their people, shaping the destiny of generations to come, not just in the tribes of Africa but across humanity itself. Today was the day Ogunwale and Ayisha had long awaited—the dawn of the fourth moon. Their wedding day.

On this sacred morning, Ayisha awoke with a radiant smile, the kind only a woman on the brink of destiny could wear. She took a deep breath, exhaling slowly before rising to her feet. The air was still cool, carrying the lingering whispers of the Atlantic breeze. She dressed herself, then set off on the familiar two-mile path through the wooded area west of her village, as she did every morning. The trail led to the shores of the Atlantic, where the sand stretched pure and white, interrupted only by the occasional scuttle of crabs or seaweed washed ashore from the night's tide. It was here, in this sacred place, that Ayisha prayed. Here, she offered her devotion to the ancestors through the rhythm of the waves, seeking their blessings on the day that would forever change her life.

Ayisha dressed in her customary yellow and white, the colors her ancestors required of her. Her white skirt, handmade with care, was sewn from cloth her father had acquired through trade with African nations to the east. Her top, short-sleeved and adorned with shades of yellow and green, was crafted from fabrics gathered from across the continent, embroidered with black crescent moons and green five-pointed stars —a tribute to the heavens. Her head was always covered, wrapped in a solid yellow scarf that concealed her thick, tightly coiled red hair. This was how Ayisha dressed each morning when she walked to the ocean. It was a sacred tradition that her ancestors had entrusted to her to bring luck and protection to the village.

But today felt different. Today looked different. Even the sway of the trees and the melody of the birds carried a strange new rhythm. The air was crisper than she had ever known it to be. For all the mornings she had walked this coastline alone, this would be her last. By nightfall, when the sun dipped beyond the horizon and the soft, gentle glow of the fourth moon took its place in the heavens, she would no longer walk in solitude. For the first time, she would make that sacred journey beside the man she had loved long before their courtship had begun.

As a little girl, Ayisha had dreamed of being with Ogunwale. He, too, had called her his wife when they were just five years old, playing in the soft white sands of the beach. Their love seemed destined by the heavens, ordained before they had even chosen their parents. As the cool mist from the waves embraced her, she envisioned herself standing as a bride, soon to be crowned a queen.

The next morning, Ayisha made her way to the beach as she always did, choosing the most beautiful spot to watch the horizon as the sun began its ascent. Along the way, she gathered wood from the forest and built a fire to ward off the crisp chill of the ocean breeze. As she sat, gazing into the rising sun, she reached for an African headdress—one that had belonged to her mother.

She lifted the yellow, red, and green garments and placed them into the fire, watching as the flames burned hotter than ever before. A deep longing settled within her as memories surfaced—her mother's final words, their last moments together before she returned to the ancestors.

"Mother, I thank you for being my mother and for all that you have taught me," Ayisha said, tears streaming down her face.

"You're welcome, my daughter. It was my pleasure to be your mother," her mother replied with a soft smile. "There is so much I need to tell you, but I can't."

Ayisha's brow furrowed. "What do you mean?"

"I have no time," her mother whispered. "But my story is your story, and while I cannot finish it, you can."

Frustration mingled with sorrow in Ayisha's voice. "Mother, all my life you have spoken in secrets and riddles. Just this once, say what needs to be said."

"Destiny will reveal what you need to know, and destiny knows more than I," her mother said gently. "When destiny comes for you, so will I. We will see each other again."

Ayisha swallowed hard, struggling to understand. "I don't fully know what you mean, but I trust that your words will come to pass. I will not fear the future or the past."

Her mother took a deep breath and placed a headdress in Ayisha's hands. "Take my headdress. Burn it on the day you step into womanhood, and keep me in your prayers."

Ayisha shook her head. "But Mother, no… This is the headdress you said the King gave you as a gift to welcome you to the village."

Her mother nodded solemnly. "Yes, daughter, that was then, but this is now. It is just another secret that must be burned."

She hesitated before adding, "But I do have one more gift for you before my time here ends. Go to your room and look under your bed. There is a door. Climb down, and retrieve what is yours."

"What is it that I am looking for?" Ayisha asked, her voice trembling.

"It is a drum," her mother said. "One made by my own hands. It is wrapped in sacred snakeskin. Hold it tightly and pass it down to the generations that follow."

Tears streamed down Ayisha's cheeks as she screamed for her mother. Her vision blurred as her eyes opened and shut, desperate to wake from the nightmare. "Mother, please! Mother, please! What will I do without you?"

"You are all that I have."

"I don't know how to finish what you are speaking of," Ayisha sobbed. "How is this drum supposed to help me?"

Her mother's voice softened, yet held an unshakable certainty. "No, Ayisha, you have more than you know. You will finish it. You shall finish it. You will finish it."

As the sun rose above the horizon, the fire burned down to embers, leaving behind only ashes where Shekhinah's headdress once lay. The cinders barely glowed, the remnants of a ritual now complete.

Her mother had always told Ayisha that she was special—chosen to serve a purpose beyond her understanding. Ayisha never questioned it, believing that when the time was right, her destiny would reveal itself. She had, however, often asked about her father. She never knew his name or had seen his face. All she knew was that he had been a great man and that his identity had to remain a secret to protect her life.

But on this glorious day, none of those questions mattered. Today, she was not concerned with the mysteries of her past or the weight of her destiny. Today, she would become Princess Ayisha, and all she could think about was how she would look in her wedding dress.

As she walked back from the beach, a sense of fulfillment settled over her. She had completed one of the tasks her mother had asked of her on the day she became a woman. Entering the royal quarters, she found the Queen and thirteen of her attendants waiting to prepare her for the wedding.

For this special day, Ayisha bathed in the finest oils and the purest, freshest water the kingdom had to offer. Her wedding dress had been sewn by hand over the course of eight months, crafted from rare silk imported from a far eastern country with which the Ebonee Kingdom often traded. This silk was so rare that it was produced in only three places in the world.

In addition to the silk, the dress was adorned with delicate lace, intricate beadwork, and elaborate embroidery. Every embellishment had been placed with care, creating the perfect gown for the perfect day.

Ayisha's dress was sewn and meticulously tailored by the finest needlewomen in the kingdom. The gown was a striking scarlet red with accents of black and green, cut to fit the curves the Creator had blessed her with. It shimmered with glistening yellow crystals, sparkling white pearls, and exquisite beadwork, each detail designed to reflect the richness of her culture and the legacy of the kingdom.

More than a garment, Ayisha's wedding dress was a masterpiece, a tribute to the craftsmanship and artistry of the designers who brought it to life. The intricate patterns and carefully sewn details held deep cultural significance, making the gown the heart of the traditional African wedding ceremony. It was more than just a display of regal beauty—it was a symbol of honor, a way to pay tribute to her ancestors and the heritage that defined her people.

Although her dress was breathtaking, fitting her like a second skin, the true centerpiece of her attire was her headdress. Before her mother's passing, she had designed it specifically for this day. Shaped like a crown, it was crafted from the gleaming, malleable metals found in the southern regions of the African continent. Her crown was adorned with thirteen jewels that shimmered and danced under the sunlight. Six deep red rubies and six bright green emeralds lined the sides in alternating fashion—each ruby beside an emerald. At the very top, resting at the center of her forehead, was a magnificent thirteen-carat diamond, its brilliance unmatched.

Fully dressed in her royal wedding attire, Ayisha was escorted to the river's edge and placed aboard the royal ferry. Its destination was a man-made island at the river's widest point. As the ferry drifted away from the mainland, Ayisha turned back for one final look at the kingdom—the land she had always known, the place she would leave behind as an ordinary woman. The next time her feet touched the mainland, she would be Princess Ayisha. The river breeze lifted her dress, sending it billowing in every direction, but nothing could erase the smile that seemed permanently etched on her face.

As the ferry neared the island, the rhythmic pounding of ceremonial drums and the harmonious voices of the kingdom filled the air. The assembled crowd sang in celebration, their chants rising to greet the bride and princess as she arrived on the island's shores.

Standing on the elaborately decorated ferry, Ayisha could hear the voices of her people lifting in unison, their melodies blending with the deep, steady pulse of the drums. On the shore, Obatala waited patiently to exchange vows, his presence regal against the backdrop of the jubilant assembly.

The tenor voices of the men rang out, chanting, "Ogunwale Kupanda! Ogunwale Kupanda!"—Ogunwale, rise! In Swahili. In response, the women of the Ebonee Kingdom sang with pride, their voices carrying over the water, "Ayisha nyota nzuri, nyota nzuri Ayisha!"—Ayisha, beautiful star!

As the villagers chanted the names "Ogunwale and Ayisha" to the rhythmic beats of the drums, the soulful melodies wove through the gathering, uniting guests in a shared sense of joy and reverence. The vibrant hues of traditional African attire adorned the attendees, their colors adding to the breathtaking spectacle of the wedding. Swaying with the river breeze, the people danced in harmony with the enchanting rhythm of the drums, their movements an extension of the celebration itself.

The voices that sang out "Ogunwale" and "Ayisha" carried the spirit of the occasion—a union of past and present, tradition and the promise of a future yet to unfold. The four neighboring tribes—the Trader Tribe, the Tribe of the Waterways, the Tribe of the Gatekeepers, and the Tribe of the Orisha—had all gathered to honor and celebrate the new royal bride and groom.

The drumming and singing ceased, giving way to an eerie stillness as Ogunwale and Ayisha stepped forward, hand in hand. The kingdom's spiritual leader stood before them, his voice solemn as he recited the sacred rites, calling upon the gods to bless this momentous day.

But for Ayisha, the moment was both joyous and heavy, sweet and sorrowful.

Tears streamed down her face as childhood memories flooded her mind—their carefree days running along the beach, laughter mingling with the sound of crashing waves, the innocent promises whispered in the sand. This was the day she had always dreamed of, the day she had always imagined her mother would witness. Yet deep in her heart, Ayisha knew the truth. Her mother was not here in flesh—only in spirit, watching from beyond.

As the final blessings were spoken, Ayisha gazed up at her new husband—her soon to be king, the man she had loved and trusted her whole life. He stood before her, tall and proud, the embodiment of everything she had dreamed of. Her heart swelled with joy, yet something in his eyes made her pulse quicken. A shadow flickered there, a quiet unease settling deep in her chest.

She smiled, but a nagging sensation churned in the pit of her stomach—a warning she couldn't quite place. Their eyes locked, and her heart fluttered with affection for the man who had always been her world. But deep within Ogunwale's heart, love had already been eclipsed.

Beneath the facade of devotion, his heart no longer belonged to her. He no longer saw Ayisha, the girl he had once cherished. His gaze was fixed on something far more dangerous, far more intoxicating. Power.

Ambition coiled around his soul, suffocating what remained of the boy she had known. His mind was consumed with conquest, with a hunger for dominion over all five nations. His thirst for control had swallowed any remnants of love he had once held for her.

Ayisha was no longer his queen. She was a piece on the board—a pawn in a game far greater than she could ever comprehend. And Ogunwale would stop at nothing to win.

Her smile faltered for only a moment, but Ogunwale didn't notice. His mind had already moved ahead, calculating the next step in his grand design—the one that would unite the nations under his rule, without Ayisha by his side.

As she stood there, blissfully unaware of the storm brewing within him, a quiet dread crept in, trailing her like a shadow. This was the happiest day of her life, but she had no idea how quickly that joy would slip through her fingers, unraveling with a force neither of them could have foreseen.

"So, he knew Ayisha was his sister and still married her? Why?" Ishmael asked, disbelief lacing his voice.

"Because the truth of who she was twisted something dark inside him," the grandmother replied, her tone steeped in ancient wisdom. "It filled him with hate, with spite."

"He was jealous," Eshe whispered, barely audible. "Jealous of what she was destined to become."

The grandmother nodded. "Envy and hatred—those are the most poisonous emotions a heart can hold. The most sinful."

"That's how it begins," Eshe continued, her voice filled with sorrow. "The fever, the rage...that burning sense of powerlessness. It's what turns even the purest souls into something cruel, something unrecognizable."

Ogunwale was never the same afterward, not once he'd discovered the true nature of his bride. The truth shattered him, dismantling everything he had once been.

"From that moment," Eshe spat, her words sharp as a blade, "he became a man driven by blood and ambition, consumed by an endless hunger for power. Nothing—and no one—was sacred. He would destroy anyone, anything, to take what he believed was rightfully his. No remorse. No mercy."

CHAPTER 10

"THE KING'S HIDDEN DARKNESS"

After the wedding, Ogunwale set his plan in motion, secretly plotting to become the ruler of all five nations, with the Kingdom of Ebonee as the spearhead of his conquest. He sought to dismantle the fragile peace among the four neighboring nations, believing that a single king should govern them all under his absolute authority.

Ogunwale became increasingly drawn to the wisdom of the old medicine woman, seeking her counsel whenever he needed guidance. It was she who first planted the idea in his mind—not just to rule his kingdom, but to reign over all the lands. One evening, under the veil of darkness, she revealed a terrible truth: if his father succeeded in exposing the secrets surrounding Shekhinah's death to the five nations, everything Ogunwale had built would collapse. There was only one solution. King Obatala had to die.

Ogunwale knew that killing his father would not be easy, but he was willing to make the sacrifice to see his vision fulfilled. And on a night thick with storm clouds, as the firelight cast eerie shadows across the medicine woman's hut, she whispered the words that would forever alter his fate. A seed of deceit was planted in his mind—a seed so dark, so corrupting, that it took root deep within him, changing the man he once was.

"You must accept the challenge I am about to offer you, young king."

"You must become more than a man, more than a king. You must become something the world has never seen before."

Ogunwale frowned. "What do you mean, elder one?"

The old woman's voice dropped to a whisper. "To defeat your father and unite the surrounding tribal nations under your rule, you must become a 'dark one'—a shadow king."

Ogunwale let out a sharp laugh. "A shadow king?" He scoffed. "Are you mocking me, old woman? I have never heard such blasphemy before!"

The old woman's expression hardened. She raised her hand to strike him for his insolence, but Ogunwale's reflexes were swift. He caught her wrist in midair, his grip tightening with barely restrained fury. His pulse pounded, his blood boiling with anger.

A slow smile spread across the woman's face. "Yes, young king, that is the fire you need to defeat your father. Anger is your gift. We will use it to shape you into something greater than you are now."

Ogunwale's breath came in heavy bursts, but gradually, he exhaled, his pulse slowing.

The old woman leaned in. "Do you trust me, young king? Have I not spoken the truth thus far?"

He hesitated, then bowed his head. "Yes, you have. And I apologize for my ignorance. Please… guide me." His voice was laced with regret, yet a new determination burned in his eyes.

Ogunwale harbored ill intentions toward his father and the kingdom. In secret, he plotted to shatter the fragile peace among the four neighboring nations and claim the throne as ruler over all five. He sought a way to bring them under a single dominion—his. If his plan succeeded, every king of the five nations would kneel beneath his authority.

But first, he had to conquer the Kingdom of Ebonee, the strongest of them all.

Betrayal weighed on his mind. To wage war against his people would mark him as a traitor, yet his ambition burned hotter than his conscience. He wrestled with the thought, but the hunger for power gnawed at his reasoning, threatening to consume him whole.

Days later, the medicine woman gathered the priests, mystics, and wise men from across the five nations—those who knew of the plot and swore allegiance to it.

A grand ceremony was performed. Encircling Ogunwale, they called upon the dark forces of the ancestral realm. They anointed his body with ancient potions, their voices rising in rhythmic chants, binding him in spells whispered through centuries. Then, without hesitation, they sent him into the dark, barren forest in the northern reaches of his kingdom—where no man returned unchanged.

The young king walked for seven days without food or water. He was delirious and weak until he stumbled upon a recluse's cavern. Obatala entered the cave, passing all the creatures that lurked within, patiently awaiting him. They stared at him with vacant eyes, their gaze filled with a darkness so profound it seemed to mirror the deepest corners of the human soul.

Ogunwale lay buried in a shallow grave, his arrival long anticipated. Earth was piled upon him until the stale, suffocating air of the cave could no longer reach his lungs. He lay there, drained of all strength, until his final breath slipped away. For seven minutes, the tomb remained silent. No movement, no whisper of sound—only the oppressive stillness of that grave. The chamber gave no sign of life, no flicker of energy.

For seven minutes, Ogunwale was enveloped in darkness as thirteen ancestral spirits loomed over him. These spirits, bound to ancient pacts, stood ready to aid Ogunwale in shattering the fragile peace among the four neighboring nations. His ambition was clear—one kingdom under a single ruler. If he succeeded, all five kings would bow beneath his reign.

He wanted all five nations under his authority. His primary target was the kingdom of the Ebonee Nation—the strongest among them all. But conquering it would mean turning against his people. It would be an unforgivable act, a betrayal that clawed at his conscience. Yet, as his ambition grew, something darker crept within him, slowly consuming what little reason remained.

The spirits, unseen but ever watchful, hovered over the dark ceremony. Their cold eyes pierced through the night, their presence pressing against the boundaries of the living world. One by one, they sank to their knees in eerie unison, their movements precise, deliberate, tightening the circle around Ogunwale's still form. The air thickened, charged with an unsettling force, a foreboding sign of what was about to unfold.

All at once, the dirt trembled with a faint stir. Ogunwale, once lifeless, began to shift. The grip of death that had held him moments ago loosened, pulling him back into the realm of the living.

Suddenly, he bolted upright, rising to his feet without using his hands. As he emerged from the shallow grave, nothing human remained of Ogunwale. The hunger and thirst that had plagued him before his burial were gone. His eyes blazed like burning rubies, stripped of all trace of mortality. He stood there, tall, polished, and eerily flawless. But beneath that smooth, gleaming exterior, there was nothing. No soul. No remnants of the man he had been. Ogunwale was no more. He was reborn as the Shadow King.

The Shadow King had only one purpose—to kill, to maim, to consume every shred of power within his reach. His thirst for destruction was endless, a hollow void that could never be filled. Rising from the depths of his grave, he returned with a fury so intense it twisted the very air around him. The ground beneath him trembled, as though even the earth feared his presence.

He was no longer a man. He was something darker, something relentless—an unyielding force determined to reshape the future. And the future would bow to him alone.

Reborn to bring destruction, he moved with a singular purpose— to establish his absolute rule. The world would tremble beneath his reign, and no force, no soul, could stand in his way. His presence spread across the land like a slow, creeping poison, darkening everything in its path. With every step, the shadows thickened, pressing down like an unshakable force. The rule of one king was inevitable. But the price would be too terrifying to imagine. The future would be written in blood.

CHAPTER II

"THE DARK DECEIT OF MAN"

King Ogunwale sat in the quiet of his war room, the dim candlelight casting restless shadows along the cold stone walls. The crown upon his brow felt heavier than ever, pressing into his skull like an iron vice, suffocating his thoughts. He had fought, bled, and slaughtered for his throne. His kingdom had never been stronger, yet a deep hunger gnawed at him—one that conquest could no longer satisfy. His vision had outgrown the borders of his land. To rule all, to bend the very earth to his will, he had to make sacrifices. And the price was steep. The cost of his ambition had come in the form of his beloved wife, Queen Aiysha, and the monstrous truth he had buried deep within himself— she was not just his queen. She was his sister.

The realization twisted in his gut. Aiysha had always been at his side—his equal, his closest confidante. Together, they had crushed their enemies and forged an unshakable reign. But now, her beauty and nobility had become a curse. She was the key to his future, but only if he was willing to betray her completely.

The thought consumed him. Aiysha was the one who could grant him the power he sought, for in the eyes of the foreign slave traders, her worth was beyond measure. With her sale, he would secure the wealth and weaponry needed to shatter the four neighboring kingdoms that dared to challenge him. His pulse quickened. His gaze drifted into the shadows. He knew what had to be done. The choice was clear. And it made his blood run cold.

Night after night, Ogunwale met in secret with the European traders, the weight of his decision pressing heavier with each passing moment. Their whispers spoke of gold—wealth beyond imagination—and weapons so powerful they could shift the balance of any war. However, to Ogunwale, these transactions were merely a means to an end. Darkness crept into his every thought, consuming the remnants of his hesitation. Aiysha's face haunted him long after the meetings ended. She trusted him. She loved him. How could he betray her so completely? But the more he dwelt on the power that awaited him, the more her life seemed insignificant. Her fate had been sealed the moment he allowed himself to entertain this treacherous deal.

He could already taste the intoxicating thrill of dominance, and it drowned out the whispers of his conscience. The burden of the crown had never felt so suffocating.

Ogunwale's hands trembled as he clutched the edges of the cold stone table, his knuckles white against the unforgiving surface. The candlelight cast restless, twisting shadows across his face, distorting the expression of the man he once was. The war room was silent, yet he heard nothing but the relentless thudding of his heart, hammering against his ribs, drowning out every last voice of reason. The air was thick with the scent of burning wax, but it did little to soothe the storm raging inside him.

He had built his kingdom on blood and fire, crushing his enemies and seizing their lands. His empire stretched farther than any before him, his rule unchallenged. Yet it was slipping through his fingers like sand. He had sworn to protect her, to cherish her. And yet, in his mind, all he could see was Aiysha—his sister, the woman he once vowed to love—bound and sold for a price.

The hours dragged on, stretching into an eternity as Ogunwale's thoughts twisted in on themselves, ensnaring him in a storm of desire and guilt. The slave traders' promises echoed in his mind—gold, weapons, an army that no force could defeat. They whispered of glory, of an unshakable reign. He could feel their words burrowing deep, feeding the hunger that clawed at his soul.

Yet with every thought of power, every vision of his enemies crushed beneath his heel, Aiysha's face burned through the haze of his ambition. Her eyes, full of trust, full of love, pierced through the darkness overtaking him. He had grown numb to her presence, to her touch. He had steeled himself, convinced that this was for the good of the kingdom, for the future of their people. But beneath all his justifications, the truth festered.

This was not for the kingdom. It was for himself. His empire. His legacy. And it was worth more than the woman who had stood by his side.

That night, as the moon hung low in the sky, Ogunwale paced his chambers, his mind a battlefield. The final meeting with the European traders was upon him. The plan was set, the deal nearly sealed. Queen Aiysha would be taken from the palace, her absence disguised beneath the veil of diplomacy. And in the dead of night, the traders would claim her. She would be bound, shackled, and sold to a fate more brutal than he dared to imagine. The very thought twisted his gut, yet the vision of wealth and power kept his feet moving forward. His heart was a war zone, torn between the woman who had loved him and the throne that promised him dominion over all. Redemption was beyond his reach now—he had strayed too far into the abyss. There would be no turning back. As the hour crept closer, an icy chill crawled up his spine, the weight of his decision pressing in from all sides. The power he sought was so close he could taste it—yet it was already slipping through his grasp. The price of betrayal had begun to consume him from within.

The plan was nearly complete. Tomorrow night, when the moon was nothing more than a sliver in the sky, Aiysha would be sent on a diplomatic mission—a convenient lie to steal her away from the palace and deliver her into the hands of the slave traders. In the dead of night, as the kingdom lay still beneath the stars, they would come for her. She would be shackled, bound, and sold into a lifetime of suffering—her existence reduced to nothing more than a transaction, a sacrifice for Ogunwale's insatiable hunger for power. His heart pounded as the weight of his betrayal pressed in on him. The very blood that tied them together, the bond they once shared, had now become the chain that would seal her fate. His kingdom. His legacy. They were all that mattered now. To lose them would mean losing everything. To claim them, he would sacrifice everything—even the woman he had once loved.

But as the hour approached, doubt crept in like a cold, relentless fog. Ogunwale stood alone on his balcony, gazing out at the kingdom he had built—the kingdom he was about to destroy. The wind whispered through the trees, carrying the faintest trace of Aiysha's laughter. It mocked him, twisting the knife deeper into his conscience. Was this the moment when everything would fall apart? The thought clung to him like an unseen hand, tightening its grip with each passing second. His ambition had burrowed deep within him, but was it worth the price of his soul? The weight of his decision pressed down on him. His rule had been forged in blood, but this—this would be the ultimate betrayal. There would be no turning back. As the night stretched on, the unease gnawed at him, its grip growing deeper. And in that moment, Ogunwale felt a chill crawl down his spine as a terrible realization took hold. The throne he sought might already be lost.

CHAPTER 12

"AN IDENTITY LOST"

As she stood chained on the deck of the European ship alongside 150 other captured Africans, Issabella's thoughts spiraled. Her new "master" stepped into view—a tall, middle-aged man with a thick head of hair, his features blurred in her memory. Just another stranger. Just another monster to endure. But she had no time to dwell on him; she was too busy trying to keep her composure, clinging to the last shred of dignity as her husband turned away. He didn't even look at her—his eyes averted in shame—while her world was ripped away. And yet, despite the storm of emotions raging inside her, one truth remained inescapable: she was at his mercy.

The white man slowly approached Aiysha, his suffocating stench making her recoil. His cold, pale hand clamped around her jaw, and his piercing gray eyes seemed to cut through her very soul. "Listen carefully," he sneered. "You need to understand this: you are my property, and you will obey my commands the moment I give them." He leaned in, his voice dripping with cruelty. "From this moment on, you are no longer permitted to use your African name. Your name is now Issabella. If I hear you speak that name again, I will shoot you on the spot. Do you understand me?"

"Yes, I do."

"It's supposed to be 'Yes, sir, master!' Say it. Repeat after me: 'Yes, sir, master.'"

"Yes, master, I understand, master."

Having been sold by her husband, she could no longer call herself by the name her mother had given her—Aiysha. Her new identity was Issabella, named after the late grandmother of the ship's captain. She had become the captain's property, stripped of freedom, dignity, and any hope for the future.

As the ship moved through the choppy waves of the Atlantic, the chill of the ocean breeze whispered against Issabella's skin, its touch almost spectral as it wove through her hair and drifted over her face, seeping into every hidden space beneath the thick, traditional shawl clinging tightly to her body. She inhaled deeply, drawing in the sharp, salty scent of the sea—the same scent that had haunted her for months. The ocean stretched before her, a vast expanse of turquoise and green, bathed in the eerie glow of the blood-orange setting sun. It was beautiful, undeniably so, but it brought no comfort. Not anymore.

The stillness of the horizon almost lulled her into forgetting the memory that had been burned into her soul. But then came the truth, cutting through the fragile calm like a blade. You never forget your first storm.

Issabella's eyes drifted shut, and the memory surged forward, relentless and consuming, like a monstrous wave battering a fragile boat. Six months had passed since that hellish journey began, yet the wound it left had never closed. The pain, raw and unyielding, refused to fade. It was as if the storm still raged inside her, buried deep within her core, never relenting. The scar it left on her soul was one that time could never erase.

The journey had been long and merciless. They had not understood the silence of the sea, its deceptive beauty. She had watched, helpless, as bodies were thrown overboard—victims of starvation, disease, or the unforgiving ocean itself. The young, the hopeful—all reduced to numbers, mere bargaining chips for men without mercy. Six months of suffering had led to its final destination: Alabama. A place that should have meant safety, a chance to rest. Instead, it was another graveyard, where those who survived were too broken to fight. Issabella had been one of the few who endured, dragging her exhausted body to shore—battered, hollow, with nothing left but rage.

But it wasn't just the storm that haunted her. It was the day everything changed—the day she lost it all. The day her husband, the man who had once sworn to protect her, condemned her to a fate worse than death. His eyes had refused to meet hers, clouded with guilt as he handed her over to the slave traders, as though she were nothing more than property. His betrayal cut deeper than any wound. She had no voice, no power to resist. Her tears burned—not just with grief, but with fury. It was not just sorrow that filled her. It was rage—deep, unrelenting, a fire that had smoldered within her since the moment he let her go.

Upon arriving at the Freeman plantation, deep in the stifling heat of southern Alabama, Issabella was confronted by the harsh reality of her new life. The plantation stretched endlessly before her—two hundred acres of barren cotton fields, their rows forming an unbroken prison under the unforgiving sun. The moment her feet touched the dry, cracked earth, the world she had once known seemed to disappear, swallowed by fear and isolation.

Without a word, she was directed toward the fields, her heart sinking with each reluctant step. The overseer, a towering man with a jagged scar running down his cheek, didn't spare her a second glance. His cold, unwavering gesture pointed to the cotton, and with it, her fate was sealed. She was no longer a woman with a name, no longer someone with dignity or a past worth remembering. She was nothing more than a tool—bound to toil beneath the ruthless sun, with no hope of escape.

Her hands, raw and trembling from the long, brutal journey, met the sharp, unforgiving cotton bushes. The air was thick with humidity, heavy with the scent of earth and sweat, suffocating her with every breath. Each movement was a battle—slow, deliberate—as she tore the cotton from the thorn-laden branches. The monotony of the task numbed her mind, each pull of the white fibers dragging her deeper into despair. The murmurs of the other workers felt distant, swallowed by the oppressive silence that smothered the fields. She recognized a few faces, but none offered solace—there was no comfort here, only the shared understanding that they were all trapped, bound by chains stronger than any that could be seen.

The days blurred together in a haze of exhaustion, each one heavier than the last. Issabella's body screamed in protest, her muscles burning, her back bent under the relentless strain. The overseer's shadow loomed over them, always present, always watching. His gaze was a silent reminder of their powerlessness, of how small and insignificant they had been reduced to. She stole glances at the other women, their eyes hollow with fatigue, yet no words passed between them, no hint of hope to share. Even the air itself seemed determined to strip them of their humanity. The promise of rest was nothing more than a cruel joke, an illusion that mocked her with its impossibility.

Nightfall brought no relief. When Issabella collapsed onto the hard, straw-stuffed mattress in the barracks, her body throbbed with pain that burrowed deep into her bones. The darkness pressed in, heavy and suffocating. The man who had sold her—his face now seared into her memory—haunted her dreams. His cold, vacant eyes, the same eyes that had stolen everything from her, lurked in the shadows of her sleep. This was her life now. There was no escape, no salvation. The cotton fields stretched endlessly before her, an unbroken expanse swallowing the horizon. And in that vast sea, she was drowning. Each day bled into the next, and the hope for freedom drifted farther away, like a whisper fading into silence.

CHAPTER 13

ESHE'S RISE TO GLORY

As Grandmother Eshe's breath grew shallow, her words barely more than whispers, a heavy stillness settled over the room. Time itself seemed to pause, as though the world held its breath alongside her. Her frail body remained tense, bracing for what was inevitable—the passage into the ancestral realm.

She spoke softly, yet her words carried the weight of generations. "You now hold the power to change everything," she rasped, her voice trembling with urgency and resolve. "Be intentional in your steps, diligent in your thoughts. Beware, child—the enemy lurks within."

Her chest rose and fell in labored breaths, but she pressed on, each word costing her more than the last. "The drum holds the power to shift everything—from the past to the present, shaping what is to come. Never forget the one true Creator of the heavens and the Earth. And beware the deceiver, who whispers sweet lies to lead you astray. Subdue your desires, resist your ambitions, for they are traps in disguise," she urged, her voice weakening, yet unwavering in its intensity.

Ishmael, his heart pounding, leaned forward. "Grandmother," he asked, his voice tight with urgency. "What is the secret of the drum?

We've done everything you've asked—we've acquired it. What does it truly hold? What is this grand mystery it contains?"

A low chuckle escaped her lips, frail and tinged with a sorrow that could not be masked. "Ah, the drum..." she sighed, her eyes gleaming with something ancient and knowing. "The drum has always been about you, Ishmael. About your lineage. That is its secret. It is tied to your destiny, to the very essence of your being. Your blood and your DNA are connected to the originator of the heavens and the Earth. Within you lies the power to shape reality itself, to bend the world to your will, if you so desire."

Her words settled in the air, heavy with meaning. "The drum... is about time," she whispered, urgency creeping into her tone. "A second chance to correct the wrongs of the past."

Ishmael's heart stuttered. "Some things?" he echoed, disbelief and intrigue warring in his voice.

Eshe's eyes clouded over for a moment, grief flickering in their depths. "Yes," she murmured, barely able to keep them open. "Only some things can be changed. But not everything. Some things must remain as they are to maintain the balance between our world and the spiritual realm. There are forces at work, Ishmael—forces older than time itself. Not all things are meant to be altered."

Her breath faltered as she gasped for air, her words draining the last of her strength, pulling her closer to the edge of the beyond. "The drum is your gateway... to this power... to this chance for change," she whispered, her voice barely audible. "Test it. Use your science, your knowledge. The key lies within you—within your blood, your very essence."

She paused, a fleeting but fierce spark of life igniting in her eyes. "Make it work. I believe in you. I know you can finish it. You can. You shall. You will."

A heavy silence filled the room as her frail body trembled with the effort to speak. "One more thing, Ishmael..." she whispered, clinging to the last thread of life. "I will always be with you. Always... live forever. And to God be the glory."

As her final breath slipped from her lips, the room seemed to exhale with her. The family rushed to her side, hands trembling as they reached for her, tears spilling freely down their faces. The moment they had feared had arrived. Grandmother Eshe, Queen of the Freeman line, had passed into the realm of the ancestors.

With a final, peaceful stillness, her body relaxed. Her hands, once clenched in a tight grip, slowly unfurled. The family's mourning gave way to a heavy, unspoken silence. Grandmother Eshe had left the world of the living, her spirit now among the ancients, watching over them from beyond.

The family prayed in a hushed reverence, their voices a gentle murmur as they prepared Eshe's body. The twins carefully draped her in all-white garments, each fold sprinkled with holy water, oil, and salt—blessings woven into every touch, every whispered prayer, and every tear shed in love.

Hours passed, and the room settled into an eerie stillness. The sobs had faded, the voices softened, yet the air remained thick with grief—and with something else. An unsettling awareness lingered, a quiet knowing that something had shifted, that something had been set into motion. The family believed in their hearts that Eshe was at peace, but the air still carried the weight of unfinished work.

For Issabella and Ishmael, that work had only just begun.

As the last of the mourners stepped away, their figures slowly dissolving into the dimness, the siblings exchanged a glance, one filled with unspoken understanding. The prophecy had not ended. It had only begun.

"Are you ready, brother?" Issabella's voice cut through the stillness, low but urgent.

Ishmael nodded, his gaze steady with purpose. "Yes, sister," he replied. "I am ready. Let us see what the past holds. Let us see what can be changed. We will resurrect a new future—not just for ourselves, but for all of us."

He paused, his voice growing firm, resolute. "We will not fear. We will not fall to temptation. And to God be the glory."

With that, the siblings moved swiftly, separating from the mourning family. They descended into the basement, their steps quick, their hearts heavy with purpose. The path ahead was uncertain, but one truth remained: the drum had spoken. And now, they would fulfill their prophecy.

Perhaps, in doing so, they would rewrite the very course of their world.

CHAPTER 14

"THE RITUAL"

Issabella and Ishmael sat in front of the drum, captivated by the mysteries of its presence and the mystique of Grandmother Eshe's story. Every seemingly insignificant event in their lives had led them to this pivotal moment.

The serpent drum was unlike anything they had ever seen. Its surface bore intricate carvings of ritualistic ceremonies and celestial beings. It rested before them in complete silence, its presence commanding. The top was rough, yet its edges were smooth where the lambskin stretched over the wood. At the center, where drummers placed their hands to summon rhythms, lay the phallus and the chalice—ancient symbols of man and woman, perfectly carved into the wood.

The engravings, about three inches deep, were filled with a dark, reddish-brown substance, giving the impression that the ancient symbols were on the verge of leaping from the drum's surface.

The snakeskin was wrapped flawlessly around the drum, without a single gap or imperfection. It was as if the serpent itself had coiled around it, binding its essence into the instrument. The black scales, sleek and polished, shimmered under the dim light, casting reflections in the eyes of Issabella and Ishmael.

When the twins won the serpent drum at the auction, the curator—an elderly man with an extraordinary knowledge of ancient relics—had told them that ancient tribes once used the drum to commune with the spirits of their ancestors. He had warned them of its power and the potential consequences of awakening the spirits that slumbered within. The curator also possessed an intimate esoteric understanding of the drum and had strongly warned them of its intoxicating vanity. He spoke in hushed tones, as though even mentioning the drum might awaken something best left undisturbed. "This drum," he had said, "was used by ancient tribes to communicate with the spirits of their ancestors. But be warned, children. The spirits you summon may not always be friendly. They do not take kindly to being disturbed from their eternal rest."

It was a warning they had heard but had not fully understood—until now. The weight of his words clung to the air, a lingering reminder of the unseen consequences they might soon face.

Ishmael and Issabella had prepared the basement of their massive home for the ritual. They surrounded themselves with candles and burning incense, filling the air with a thick haze of anticipation. They had studied blood séances in their research—rituals where blood was used to strengthen the connection between the living and the dead. It was a dangerous endeavor, but they were determined to uncover the mysteries hidden within the drum.

With the instructions for the drum in Ishmael's hands and their grandmother's wisdom embedded deep in their consciousness, they were ready to proceed with the ritual and whatever future it would bring.

Ishmael stepped toward the cabinet where his family had stored the antiques they had collected over the generations. From inside, he retrieved the Nboge sword. The Nboge was the fiercest and most feared weapon in all of Africa's ancient battles. Only five of these swords remained in modern times, and the Freeman family possessed two of them.

Gripping the sword tightly in his left hand, Ishmael approached Issabella, who now wore an old slave dress she had purchased years ago from a Civil War gift shop. The faded fabric draped her form like a ghost of the past. Ishmael, too, had dressed the part—wearing male slave trousers, a simple top, and open-toed shoes. He resembled the presentation of a house servant, his attire a stark contrast to the moment's significance.

"Are you ready, sister?" he asked.

"Yes, I am, brother," she replied. "Just be gentle and don't chop my arm off," she nervously joked.

Ishmael hesitated for a moment, his grip tightening around the sword. "Before I begin, are we sure this is what we want to do?"

"Yes," Issabella answered firmly. "It is our destiny."

"Good," he nodded. "I'll see you when we get there."

Ishmael positioned the rusty blade an inch from Issabella's arm, his breath steadying as he exhaled slowly. With deliberate precision, he pressed the edge against the vein protruding from her right arm, making a clean incision. Guiding her arm toward the drum, he allowed her blood to flow into the carved symbol of the chalice. The crimson liquid spilled over the sides, streaking the dark scales as the symbol for womanhood reached its capacity.

Issabella took the blade from her brother, her grip firm as she prepared to return the ritual. She sliced a shallow cut into Ishmael's arm, guiding his blood toward the symbol for manhood, the phallus. The deep engraving filled quickly, overflowing onto the serpent-like patterns that coiled around the drum's body.

As the blood seeped into the ancient wood, the drum trembled and pulsed with an unnatural rhythm. A faint glow emerged from the carvings, illuminating the markings with an eerie, flickering light. The twins clasped hands immediately, their hearts pounding with a mixture of fear and anticipation as they began to chant the incantations they had meticulously pieced together from the ancient manuscripts Grandmother Eshe had given them before her return to the ancestors.

The air thickened, charged with an unseen force, as the drum resonated with a deep, haunting hum. Shadows stretched and twisted along the walls, moving of their own accord, and a sudden chill swept through the room. A whispering wind carried echoes of voices long since passed. Issabella and Ishmael felt it. Something had entered the room—an unseen presence that spiraled around them like an invisible current, threading through the air, watching, waiting.

Suddenly, the drum erupted in a burst of blinding light, forcing Issabella and Ishmael to shield their eyes. When they looked again, a figure stood before them—a shimmering apparition draped in garments from a bygone era. It was the spirit of an ancestor, summoned from the depths of time by the power of the drum and their blood ritual.

The spirit's voice echoed as if carried from both the past and the present, resonating deep within their souls. It spoke of ancient battles fought and lost, of love and betrayal, of wisdom passed through the ages. Each word wove together the history of their lineage, revealing truths hidden beneath centuries of silence.

Seconds stretched into eternity, yet passed in fleeting moments. The twilight of evening filtered through the windows, the full moon casting its silver glow across the room. As the spirit's form began to fade, turning translucent, it retreated into the ether of the ancestral realm. Issabella and Ishmael bowed their heads in gratitude, humbled by the knowledge they had received.

They sat in stunned silence, their eyes fixed on the serpent drum, the magnitude of its presence settling deep within them. Every moment of their lives—every seemingly insignificant event—had led them here, to this defining instant. The air was thick with the pull of something ancient and profound, as though the very walls pulsed with the energy of generations past. They had waited for this moment, prepared for it, but standing now on the edge of the unknown, the weight of their choices pressed against them.

It was dangerous. It came with risks they could not ignore. But it was their destiny. The drum held secrets, and they were determined to unlock them.

Issabella met his gaze firmly. "Yes. It is our destiny. This is the path we must walk."

Ishmael nodded slowly. "Good. Then, I'll see you on the other side," he said, his voice thick with the weight of their decision.

Silence fell over the room. The glow from the drum dimmed, and the once-living carvings stilled, their energy withdrawing into dormancy. Issabella and Ishmael remained frozen, the enormity of what had just occurred settling over them like a heavy shroud.

They had glimpsed the past—the unseen ties binding them to the generations before. But as the weight of the ritual pressed down on them, exhaustion began to take hold. Overwhelmed by the force they had summoned, their bodies gave out in unison. With a final breath, both twins collapsed onto the floor, their forms crumpling around the serpent drum.

In the stillness that followed, the drum sat in silence, its power now dormant, waiting for the next souls brave enough to summon it.

CHAPTER 15

"THE ONE WHO WILL SAVE US? (PART 1)"

When Issabella and Ishmael awoke, the suffocating heat of a cotton field clung to their skin like an iron vise. The air was thick with the scent of earth, sweat, and something else—something sharp, metallic, like blood. They gasped, instinctively reaching for each other, but as their hands met, a jarring realization struck them. Their fingers felt different—rough, callused, and stained with dirt.

The familiar warmth of their suburban home was gone, replaced by an oppressive heaviness that seeped into their bones. As their eyes adjusted, the world around them came into sharp, unforgiving focus. This was not the present. It was 1835—the height of slavery in the American South. And they stood in the heart of the Freeman Plantation. Issabella's heart pounded violently against her ribs. She looked down at herself, and the sight stole her breath. Gone were the clothes she had worn during the ritual. In their place was a threadbare cotton dress, the kind worn by enslaved women toiling under the relentless sun. The fabric clung to her damp skin, stiff and coarse.

She turned to Ishmael, but he, too, was not the brother she had known moments before. His once-clean, youthful face was streaked with dirt, his expression shadowed by a weariness that did not belong to him. His clothes—ragged, torn at the seams—hung loosely on his frame, faded from years of use. They had been thrust into the past, their souls trapped inside the bodies of two enslaved people. But whose lives had they taken? And why? The questions swirled through their minds, frantic and unanswered. Then, before they could speak, the sharp crack of a whip shattered the thick air. A white overseer's voice rang out, harsh and unforgiving, slicing through the silence like a blade.

"Move, niggers! You two better get back to work! We've got to get this cotton on these ships in a week!" the overseer bellowed; his words laced with venom.

Without thinking, they both stepped forward, but Issabella's legs trembled as she struggled to adjust to the unfamiliar weight of her body. The rhythmic, exhausting labor that had once been nothing more than an abstract history now pressed against her like a crushing force. Sweat dripped from her forehead as she bent down, lifting the burlap sack at her feet before falling into step with the others. The endless rows of cotton stretched before them, each plant waiting to be plucked, each movement a bitter reminder of the reality they had been thrust into.

Ishmael walked beside her, his expression hollow, but his steps moved in mechanical obedience, as though his body already knew what his mind refused to accept.

It didn't take long for the full horror of their situation to settle in. The twins, though linked by blood and spirit, felt as though they had been severed from their former selves. "Come on, Freemans, we got work to do," a woman's voice called out with a chuckle. "Rose and David, y'all get married and now wanna act crazy?" Issabella and Ishmael turned sharply toward the voice, confusion flashing across their faces. Rose and David?

They were no longer physically Issabella and Ishmael—they had become David and Rose Freeman, cousins to the enslaved man set to be hanged the following morning. The ritual had worked. It had dragged their consciousness back in time, forcing them into the bodies of two enslaved people on the Freeman plantation. Issabella and Ishmael were now trapped in a system designed to break both their bodies and spirits. But even as they labored under the relentless sun, their minds raced, trying to make sense of their place in a history they had only ever read about in textbooks.

They could feel the fear and pain of their new bodies, the suffering of their ancestors etched into every muscle, every bruise that blossomed beneath the overseer's whip. They were living a nightmare—one rooted in a past they couldn't escape. "We are here, Issabella. Let's complete the mission," Ishmael whispered.

"What if we're too late?" Issabella asked, breaking the silence as Ishmael gathered his thoughts.

"We are not late. Trust me, I can feel it," Ishmael insisted.

As the sun began to set, casting a dim, golden glow over the cotton fields, the twins drifted toward the edge of the plantation, their steps careful, their breaths shallow. A barn stood nearby, its doors slightly ajar, offering a temporary refuge from the approaching night.

The other enslaved workers, weary from a long day in the fields, trudged toward their quarters on the far side of the plantation. Seizing their moment, the twins slipped away from the group, their movements swift but deliberate. They ran, feet kicking up dust as they crossed from the fields to the barn, their hearts pounding against their ribs. The sun was now low in the western sky, casting long shadows across the land. Around them, the endless stretch of cotton fields swayed gently in the evening breeze. The familiar scent of earth and sweat clung to the air, grounding them in the grim reality of their mission.

As they stole a moment of quiet, the hum of the world around them faded, allowing them to catch their breath. Their eyes met, and in that shared glance, their bond was both a source of strength and sorrow. The ritual had not been placed too late, but a day early, before the lynching of their ancestor.

"We've got one shot at this. We need to save our ancestors. They're still here."

This wasn't just a journey into the past—it was a mission to change it. And it was personal. Grandmother Eshe had filled their childhood with stories of their ancestors—stories of freedom, resistance, and most importantly, love. They came from a long line of fighters, people who refused to be broken.

Issabella and Ishmael had grown up in the comfort of their lavish suburban home, never knowing the brutal reality of slavery firsthand. But they had always felt its presence in the stories their grandmother told—tales of oppression, resilience, and unbreakable family bonds. Their great-great-grandparents had been among the countless African Americans sold at auction, torn apart, and forced into bondage.

Ishmael blinked, momentarily disoriented, while Issabella was already scanning the horizon. "We've arrived. Now, we just need to wait for the moment before she's hanged in the morning."

He exhaled sharply before adding, "Let's rest here tonight so we can be fully prepared for what's to come tomorrow."

Issabella nodded. "We'll need our strength in the morning."

The twins nestled together amid the bales of hay, exhaustion settling over them like a heavy fog. Ishmael gripped a pitchfork tightly in his left hand, his fingers curling around it as if it were the only thing tethering him to this moment. As the night deepened, a blanket of darkness stretched across the land, the stars shimmering like distant beacons of hope. The barn creaked softly—a familiar sound that provided a fragile sense of comfort amidst the tension. Ishmael and Issabella lay close, their breaths rising and falling in quiet unison. The weight of the impending dawn pressed against them, each moment stretching like a taut string ready to snap.

Ishmael couldn't shake the unease gnawing at him. He glanced down at the pitchfork in his hand, its cold metal catching the dim light seeping through the cracks in the barn walls. A tool of labor, yet tonight, it felt like something else—something desperate, something necessary.

He turned to Issabella, whose eyes were closed, her brow creased in deep thought. He admired her resolve, the way she always found clarity even in the darkest of times.

"Do you think we can really change anything?" Ishmael whispered, breaking the silence.

Issabella opened her eyes, her gaze steady and unwavering. "We have to believe we can," she replied, her voice firm. "If we don't stand up for her, who will? We can't let fear dictate our actions."

Her words settled within him, igniting a quiet but unshakable determination. They were not just waiting; they were preparing to fight for righteousness, to challenge the fate that had been written in blood and fear.

"Good night, sister. Tomorrow is our day of justice. We will prevail."

CHAPTER 16

"THE ONE WHO WILL SAVE US? (PART 2)"

As the hours passed, the world outside the barn quieted down, the sounds of crickets and rustling leaves fading into a gentle lullaby. Ishmael's eyelids grew heavy, exhaustion finally overtaking him. He knew they needed rest to regain their strength for the battle ahead. With one last glance at his sister, he allowed himself to relax, the tension in his body slowly easing. During the night, dreams drifted through his mind, filled with visions of freedom—a world where justice prevailed and people stood united against oppression. He saw the young woman they fought for, her spirit unbroken despite the grim circumstances—their Ancestor.

In his heart, Ishmael knew their mission was more than saving a single life; it was about igniting a spark of change. As dawn approached, the first rays of sunlight seeped into the barn, brightening the hay and casting soft shadows around them. Ishmael stirred, feeling the heaviness of purpose pressing firmly upon his shoulders. He turned toward Issabella, her face softly lit by the early morning sun. In that moment, hope surged within him. Together, they would face whatever awaited them beyond those barn doors. The hour for action was near, and they would face it without fear.

"Today is the day of our retribution," she said, her voice steady. "We must stick to the plan. We know what we need to do." Ishmael nodded, absorbing the seriousness of her words. They had spent countless hours crafting their strategy, analyzing options, and discussing the risks. Now, their resolve would be put to the test. The gravity of the situation pressed upon them, matched only by their fierce determination to bring change.

After quickly eating the bread they had saved, the twins gathered their belongings, making sure Ishmael firmly held the pitchfork. It was more than just a tool—it symbolized their commitment to protecting the innocent and confronting the injustices they had witnessed. Quietly, they moved toward the barn doors, their footsteps softened by the hay beneath them. Sunlight streamed through cracks in the wood, brightening their path forward. But just as they were about to exit, they halted, sensing sudden danger. Heavy footsteps crunched against the gravel outside. A young white man, driven by anger and entitlement, stormed toward the barn, his face flushed with rage. He had heard rumors about enslaved people hiding there and was determined to stop their escape. At the barn entrance, he hesitated briefly, gathering himself before bursting through the door, sunlight piercing through swirling dust motes in the air.

"Come out here now, niggers! I know you're in there!" he shouted, his voice echoing off the barn walls. Ishmael felt a rush of adrenaline, his instincts sharpening as he remained silent, hoping to blend into the shadows. Issabella quietly stood behind her brother, clutching a stone she'd picked from the barn floor. A confrontation was inevitable, but neither intended to become victims like their ancestors had centuries earlier.

As the master's son moved further into the barn, tension thickened, heavy and electric, the air charged with imminent conflict. The young white man advanced slowly, his eyes narrowed, scanning the dimly lit space. "I don't need my father out here, and I'm not afraid of you niggers! You think you can just hide?" His words cut with accusation, each syllable challenging, sparking fear and fury in Ishmael. He knew in that moment he had a choice: stay hidden or face the danger directly. Grasping the pitchfork leaning against the wall, Ishmael steadied his breathing. He had every right to defend himself. As the master's son opened the barn doors wider and moved forward, a burst of courage drove Ishmael into action.

The confrontation escalated quickly from threats to a physical struggle, both young men locked in a fierce battle of willpower, the atmosphere explosive. Suddenly, events spiraled beyond control. The master's son lunged forward, aggression visible in every movement, but Ishmael reacted instinctively. Swiftly, he thrust the pitchfork forward, the prongs sinking deep into the attacker's neck.

A gasp escaped the young man's lips as he stumbled backward, shock overtaking anger as blood poured from his neck, staining his pale skin. As the master's son fell unconscious, Ishmael swiftly removed the long machete from the man's right side, preparing himself for another conflict. Issabella grabbed the pitchfork from the ground as they quickly scanned the plantation grounds. In the distance, they spotted a woman being dragged by two white men. She appeared distressed, and the swollen curve of her belly revealed she was pregnant. "That's her!" Issabella exclaimed urgently. "That's the ancestor grandmother told us about—we only have minutes before we have to go back."

"Let's save her now while we still have time," Ishmael urged. As they moved swiftly toward the hanging tree, voices rose clearly from near the lynching tree, where a local pastor preached fervently:

"I am the God of Abraham, the God of Isaac, and the God of Jacob! God is not the God of the dead, but of the living."

The twins pressed onward, footsteps determined and heavy with rage. Ishmael felt the tension spark in the air like lightning before a storm. Ahead loomed the twisted, ancient tree, roots thick and gnarled like clawing hands. It was a place where suffering had been measured in lashes, where their hopes had been crushed into the dirt beneath their feet.

The overseer stood beneath the tree, a cruel figure outlined by the faint glow of the rising sun, unaware of the storm building behind him. He had no idea what was approaching. Ishmael's heart pounded in his chest, each beat fueled by years of pain and resentment. Issabella stood firmly beside him, her expression cold and determined, as the heaviness of the moment pressed down upon them. As they neared the base of the tree, Ishmael felt his anger rise, a fury boiling from deep within his soul. He clenched his fists, nails biting into his palms, until he could no longer hold back.

With a thunderous roar, Ishmael threw his head back and released a cry of unrestrained rage—a primal shout echoing through the trees, resounding across distant hills. His voice became a weapon, a torrent of raw emotion tearing through the silence of the forest. Swiftly, he drew back the machete gripped tightly in his left hand, and with one mighty swing, he severed the overseer's head.

"You will hear me!"

The second overseer's face twisted in disbelief at the sound that seemed to shake the ground beneath him. His gaze fixed upon Ishmael, who stood tall, body tensed with the fury of a storm ready to erupt. Ishmael's shout was a declaration, announcing their presence to the world and to the oppressors who never imagined they would rise. The overseer's smug expression faltered, uncertainty flashing across his eyes. He reached for the whip at his side, but the movement was hesitant, sluggish—he had underestimated them.

Issabella surged forward, driving the pitchfork deep into the overseer's chest, sending him collapsing to the ground, life rapidly fading from his body. The wind rose, carrying Ishmael's anger outward, the forest responding as branches swayed in harmony with the fury now filling the air.

"Today," Ishmael declared, voice quiet yet powerful, "we take back what was stolen."

"Today, you answer for your cruelty."

The enslaved people who had gathered for the sermon stood frozen in silence, staring at the bloodshed before them. "What is the meaning of this, David?" Aiysha asked, her voice trembling. "Are you possessed? I've never seen you act this way. What devil has gotten into you?"

"You look like David, but you ain't him, are you?" she added, her eyes narrowing with confusion.

"Not at this moment, good sister," Ishmael replied, his voice calm but distant.

"I knew someone like you would come. Don't ask me how—I just knew," she murmured, almost to herself.

Aiysha looked at him, eyes filled with gratitude and awe. "Thank you for saving me—and my babies. We're truly blessed because of you!" She placed a protective hand over her swollen belly. "My twins will live free because of you, angels sent from God!"

"Twins?" Issabella exclaimed, surprise filling her voice.

"Yes, baby," Aiysha replied, a smile brightening her face. "I can feel their four little feet kicking all day." She laughed gently, joy radiating from her.

Before they could continue speaking, approaching footsteps interrupted them. Churchgoers had begun to arrive, drawn by whispers of the carnage they'd heard unfolding. Conversations ceased abruptly as they stared at the devastation before them. What seemed like an ordinary confrontation between two slaves had suddenly transformed into something much greater. In that moment, Issabella and Ishmael had changed their future forever.

But their time in this cruel, distant past was slipping away. Already, their consciousness was shifting, pulling them back toward their proper timeline in the future. Before Ishmael lost consciousness, drawn inevitably homeward, he spoke words that would echo through generations on the Freeman plantation:

"You are not animals. You must fight to claim your rightful place on this earth—not merely as slaves, but as men. You deserve to be seen as human beings, to be treated with the respect and dignity owed to every person. You deserve the rights of humanity—here and now, on this very day—a day we will bring about by any means necessary!"

Then, the twins collapsed into darkness, their bodies going limp as consciousness slipped away, pulling them back to the future.

CHAPTER 17

"THE GARDEN FULL CIRCLE"

As Issabella gradually regained consciousness, an eerie stillness surrounded her. The air felt different—dense with a scent reminiscent of ancient earth. Beneath her, the ground was soft and unfamiliar, its texture strangely unsettling. She remained motionless, hesitant to open her eyes, as though some hidden force might reveal itself the moment she did. The silence was broken only by the distant sounds of birds and the occasional rustling of unseen creatures. Above her, water rushed forcefully, as though the earth itself had awakened, brimming with hidden mysteries.

She hesitated, tension tightening within her chest. When she finally opened her eyes, the brightness of the sky pierced her vision sharply, forcing her to flinch.

The grass at her feet appeared impossibly green, richer than any color she had ever known. The sky was a boundless, flawless blue that seemed to stretch forever. It was as if the world had been painted by a brush untouched by imperfection. Then she saw them—the creatures. Wild and improbable animals, their shapes unlike anything she had encountered before. Their eyes observed her with a disturbing intelligence, as if they understood exactly who she was and why she had come. She slowly stood, her body weak and trembling, heart pounding with confusion and dread. She took a cautious step, then another, her senses overwhelmed by the strangeness around her. She wasn't sure where she was, but the sinking feeling inside told her that, deep down, she knew exactly where she'd ended up.

The whispers from the spirit of the drum echoed softly in Issabella's mind, faint yet insistent. She had been sent here for a purpose her brother, Ishmael, would never understand nor willingly permit. She had hidden this part of her mission from him, knowing he would only attempt to stop her, protecting her from dangers even he couldn't grasp.

The spirits of their ancestors had brought her here, back to the dawn of creation—to the Garden of Eden itself, moments before humanity's fateful fall. It was the place where a single choice had once sealed the future of humankind. But Issabella wasn't here to rewrite the past; she was here to shape what was yet to come. The spirits had provided no explicit instructions, only a charge to trust herself, to rely on her judgment, and to exercise her free will in setting things right.

Yet, the heaviness of that responsibility pressed upon her like an invisible hand. The fate of humanity rested not in the hands of gods or rulers, but solely on her. Her thoughts, her choices, her heart— these alone would decide all that was to follow. There was no divine guidance, no intervention—only the pulsing silence of eternity, waiting expectantly. The garden stretched out before her, brimming with impossible beauty, but Issabella knew not to trust its alluring surface.

Beneath this paradise's flawless appearance hid darkness, a dangerous secret waiting to be revealed. As water surged past, the wind whispered through the trees, and creatures watched quietly from the shadows, Issabella realized with a chilling certainty that her task wasn't to preserve this place—it was to determine if it should ever exist again. The fate of the world now rested in her hands, and the judgment of the future depended entirely upon the rhythm of her heart.

Issabella's gaze shifted eastward, where her true mission awaited—the Tree of Knowledge. It rose from the earth like an ancient, silent guardian, its sturdy branches dense with dark, swirling leaves in vivid shades of red, orange, and green, each hue more intense and unnatural than the last. The tree stood isolated, towering nearly forty feet high, its trunk broad and twisted, like the grasping hands of an ancient deity emerging from the earth itself. Her pulse quickened as she acknowledged the profound gravity of her purpose. She was acutely aware of the dangers ahead.

With every step toward the tree, the air thickened, the heaviness of eternity pressing against her chest. She glanced upward, captivated by the dazzling sunlight bathing the world in a golden haze. Yet, at the edge of her vision, stars lingered—bright and steady, as if they had never departed, endlessly observing her movements. Even the sky felt wrong—too radiant, overly crowded, as though an ancient presence had awakened and now observed her every action.

The creatures of Eden—animals unlike anything she'd ever encountered, beings that seemed impossible—gathered around her. They didn't scatter fearfully, as she'd anticipated. Instead, they watched attentively, their eyes glinting with quiet reverence. With each step she took, their murmurs grew into a haunting chorus, a melody vibrating through her bones. It was as though the land itself communicated gratitude and respect, the atmosphere charged with an unshakable sense that she was not alone in this moment. The rustle of leaves and the whispers of flowing water intensified, growing urgent as she drew closer to the Tree.

As Issabella stood at the edge of the great lake, her reflection shimmered gently across the water. But the face staring back wasn't her own—not entirely. The woman reflected in the lake glowed softly, her form bathed in a celestial radiance. The gentle light seemed to pulse beneath her skin, as though the sun itself had made a home inside her body. She was no longer fully human—not yet, at least. The heaviness of this realization settled over her like a shadow creeping down her back.

Her gaze shifted toward the vast, restless lake separating her from the Tree. There was no clear route across—no bridge, no straightforward way forward. Her thoughts raced anxiously. Should she swim? The water appeared dark, its surface roiling with hidden currents, and Issabella feared whatever might dwell beneath, silently waiting to strike. Yet, turning back wasn't an option. Time was slipping away. Her task had to be completed, or everything would be lost. Failure was not a possibility.

Then, as though rising from deep within the earth itself, a voice whispered into her mind—soft, ancient, yet powerful.

"Walk, my child."

Issabella froze, her blood turning to ice. Grandmother? The voice spoke again, sharper and more urgent: "Walk, child. NOW."

Fear tightened around her like a vice, but her legs moved without conscious thought. Her bare foot hovered above the water, trembling with uncertainty. Every instinct screamed at her to turn away, to find another route, but something—someone—drew her forward. Drawing a breath filled with dread, Issabella lowered her foot onto the lake. The freezing shock jolted through her like lightning. She braced herself, expecting to sink, anticipating the cold, dark depths swallowing her whole. But as her foot touched the surface, something impossible happened—the water held firm. She took another step.

The surface beneath her was solid, stable. She glanced downward, her heart pounding in her chest. It was no longer water beneath her feet but something like air, the lake parting around her like a forgotten curtain. The glow around her pulsed gently, as though reality itself was bending at her command.

A brief calm passed through her, quickly replaced by anxiety. Her heart hammered relentlessly, and she felt the burden of history pressing heavily upon her with each step across the water, confident yet cautious. An image of Christ stepping across the Sea of Galilee flashed through her thoughts, recalling the awe and disbelief of His disciples.

She sensed them all—those who had walked before her, those who had witnessed similarly impossible things.

But what had she just done? Was this the miracle she'd been sent to accomplish, or was it only the beginning of something darker? She couldn't escape the sensation that something ancient, hidden deep beneath the lake, was watching her closely, patiently awaiting its moment to rise.

The Tree of Knowledge loomed before her, the very heart of it all. With each step Issabella took, she felt the gravity of her decision bearing down on her.

Issabella reached the Tree without further obstacle, her heart thudding painfully in her chest as she approached its towering form. Her fingers brushed the thick, ancient trunk, and an electric surge of power shot through her, as though the essence of the tree itself were alive, aware of her touch. "Magnificent, isn't it?"

The voice broke the silence, deep and smooth, rippling through the air. Issabella's pulse quickened. "Who's there? Her voice trembled, betraying her unease despite her resolve. Show yourself—I command you".

With a sinuous rustle, something stirred high above. From the upper branches, a large, emerald-green serpent descended gracefully. Its scales gleamed like polished gems, glittering strangely in the harsh sunlight. Halfway down the trunk, the serpent shed its vivid green skin, revealing a sleek, glistening black form beneath, shimmering darkly like oil upon water.

"Yes, this tree is beautiful," it hissed softly, its voice smooth and entrancing. "But not nearly as magnificent as you, my child Issabella." Issabella froze, her breath catching sharply. It knows my name, she thought.

"Yes, indeed I do," the serpent replied, its voice both mocking and strangely intimate. "I've been expecting you for a long time. A very long time."

The creature drew closer, its body smoothly coiling as it descended. It appeared to smile—if a serpent could truly smile—as its eyes met hers. The air around Issabella thickened with the creature's presence, every movement slow and deliberate, like the quiet calm preceding a storm.

"What a beautiful woman you are," it hissed, its forked tongue darting quickly. "Exactly my taste. Exactly as I expected, and even more."

It crept closer, its glossy black scales glistening as it coiled down the tree. Issabella's skin prickled with a feeling of entrapment, her gaze held captive by the serpent's hypnotic stare.

Issabella stood rooted to the spot, breath tight in her chest, as the serpent began moving in ways that defied nature. Its body twisted and rolled upon the ground, as if something ancient and powerful had awakened within it. The air grew dense, alive with electric tension, while it writhed and transformed. Then, abruptly, the movements ceased. A suffocating stillness settled over the scene.

Slowly, the serpent began to rise—its form shifting before Issabella's eyes. The sleek, coiled body elongated and changed, sinuous curves reshaping into something familiar, something commanding—the undeniable form of a man. Yet more than a man—something divine.

He towered above her, nearly eight feet tall, his powerful frame sculpted with muscles shifting beneath his dark skin like liquid shadow. His thick, woolen hair flowed down to the middle of his back, deep and rich as midnight. Under the moon's silver glow, his skin shone, accentuating each taut, defined line of his physique.

The sight of him captivated her completely. He was temptation made flesh, embodying a dangerous beauty that whispered of forbidden desires—urging her toward things hidden deep within. He was everything she'd ever feared, yet everything she'd secretly longed for.

When he turned to face her, Issabella's breath caught sharply. His eyes—intense and piercing—locked onto hers, sending a chill down her spine. Without realizing it, her gaze dropped lower, tracing the powerful contours of his body until it settled on the unmistakable movement stirring there. The sight was impossible to ignore, almost as if it possessed a will of its own.

A slow, knowing smile curved across his lips as he stepped closer, his voice deep and filled with dark amusement.

"Oh, Issabella," he murmured, his words sliding smoothly like honey, dangerously sweet. "Does something catch your eye? Something…awakening your desires?"

The way he spoke her name felt like an invitation she couldn't resist. The air seemed charged with silent promises, the space between them shrinking, heavy with relentless tension. He was like nature unleashed—powerful, irresistible, and dangerously within reach.

Issabella's heart raced, breaths quick and shallow. Was this her moment of judgment? Or the beginning of something far darker?

Issabella coughed, struggling to steady herself as the massive figure of the serpent-man loomed over her. His overpowering presence filled the air with oppressive intensity, making every breath difficult. His gaze pierced Issabella, pulling her inward, as if his eyes carried an incomprehensible force. She felt cornered, unable to break free, even as every instinct screamed for escape. He moved closer, his imposing figure casting a shadow that swallowed her whole.

He extended his left hand, fingers grazing the tips of her locs, causing her to shudder involuntarily. His touch burned against her skin, sending waves of unfamiliar energy surging through her body.

"Such beautiful red hair you have," he rumbled, his voice deep and resonant, echoing with ancient authority.

Issabella flinched and instinctively withdrew, her skin prickling with discomfort. Yet she remained frozen in place, held captive by his magnetic presence.

His gaze softened, almost melancholy. "I knew someone like you, with hair like yours. Many millennia ago," he murmured, his voice distant and sorrowful. "She was the one I loved—loved freely and completely. My greatest love." He paused, and a chill raced down Issabella's spine. "But she was taken from me. Taken without reason, without mercy. All to test my loyalty."

The bitter words hung in the air, heavy with centuries of pain. Issabella could feel the anguish radiating from his voice—an ancient suffering that trembled through the ground beneath her feet. He knew her name, her bloodline, everything about her.

"I know why you're here," he growled softly.

Issabella's heart pounded fiercely. *No,* she thought defiantly, *I won't let him control me.*

"Get away from me," she snapped, voice harsh, betraying her rising fear. Every instinct screamed at her to flee, but her legs refused to obey, rooted firmly in place by the pull of his presence.

The serpent-man's lips curled into a sinister smile, his mouth twitching with dark amusement. He laughed, a low, mocking sound that reverberated through the air and sent chills crawling up her spine.

"I can help you," he whispered, voice smooth and coaxing, dangerously persuasive. "And you can help me."

He moved closer, his words hanging between them like a tempting promise. "I can make you my queen," he murmured, the power in his voice intoxicating and dangerous. "Together, we can rule this world—unrestrained, fearless. You and I, Issabella…we could reign supreme."

His offer pierced her thoughts, taking root deep within her mind. She tried to resist, to push back against the temptation, but the air thickened with his dark energy. She could sense the promise of his power moving through the atmosphere, alive and seductive. Her pulse quickened; her breaths grew shallow. This was not a being she could easily overcome. The serpent continued, his voice dripping with dark temptation. "All I ask… is for you to carry my child," he whispered, his breath hot against her skin. He stood so close now that she could feel the warmth radiating from his body.

In his hand, he held the apple—the very fruit whose forbidden bite had altered the fate of humanity. It shone beneath the moonlight, its crimson skin pulsing softly, as if it possessed a life of its own. Issabella's heart pounded wildly, drowning out her thoughts. She felt the fruit calling her, its promise tantalizingly within reach. She had to take it. She knew she must. His words offered unimaginable power—a limitless kingdom. Her mind clouded over, twisted within a fog of temptation.

"Yes," she whispered breathlessly. "Thank you."

He reached out, gently laying her down on the damp grass. The full moon above them cast a radiant, surreal glow. Issabella felt the calm presence of the lake at her side, its surface mirroring their bodies, now intimately close.

In her palm, the fruit felt dense, as if it contained the essence of creation itself. She stared down at it, unable to look away. This was the moment, the choice that would alter everything. Within her grasp was power, wisdom—the destiny of humanity contained within its delicate skin.

The serpent-man leaned over her, his lips mere inches from hers. His voice whispered seductively in her ear, dangerously persuasive. "You have what you desire, Issabella," he murmured. "Now seal our agreement with a kiss. Together, we will rule this world as we wish."

His hand slid over her body with a slow, deliberate touch, sending a shiver down her spine. Her heart pounded in her chest. She could feel the weight of her future pressing down on her. Was this the right choice? Could she trust him? Was this deal truly the key to the power and wisdom she sought? Or was it the first step toward a downfall far worse than she could imagine?

The whispers in her head grew louder, urging her forward. The serpent's voice echoed in her thoughts, relentless, pulling her deeper into his trap. Everything had led to this moment—her fate rested on this decision.

But then, from the corner of her eye, she noticed something—a glint in the grass. It was barely visible, hidden in the shadows, but Issabella's sharp instincts kicked in. She moved swiftly, her hand darting out to seize a jagged shard of rock concealed beneath the blades of grass.

The serpent was too focused on her. His breath quickened as he leaned in, his forked tongue slithering toward her lips wet with lust and desire. It was almost too late—but it wasn't.

With a surge of strength, Issabella swung the rock upward, catching him off guard. The sharp edge sliced through the air, cutting deep into his throat before he could react. His eyes widened in disbelief, pain and shock flashing across his face as blood poured from the wound. He stumbled back, collapsing in a slow, agonizing motion.

His once-muscular form began to wither, aging before her eyes as the life drained from him. His body shrank, and his strength began to fade. The serpent-man's form crumbled into nothingness, dissolving into mist and vanishing as suddenly as he had appeared.

The Garden of Eden stood silent once more. The moonlight reflected off the still lake, casting an eerie glow over the scene. The whispers of the past faded into the night.

Issabella stood trembling, the forbidden fruit still clutched in her hand. The weight of her decision pressed down on her. Was it the right choice? The fruit, now so close, seemed to hum with an ancient force, yet it felt heavier than before.

As the world around her spun, her body weakened, the edges of her vision blurring. Her legs buckled, and she collapsed, slipping into unconsciousness as the Garden returned to its eternal stillness.

And the echoes of ancient secrets… remained untouched.

For a moment, her breath caught in her throat. Then—relief. Her face stared back at her. She knew that face. She exhaled, lungs heavy with the breath she hadn't realized she was holding.

I made it…

She stepped back from the mirror, nearly stumbling, and pressed her hands against her face, grounding herself in the tangible reality around her. The mission, the prophecy, the ancient promise that had haunted her family for generations—was complete. She had done it. She was home.

But the silence was shattered as a series of knocks echoed against the bedroom door, sending a jolt through her.

Knock, knock, knock.

The door creaked open, and a familiar voice cut through the tension settling in her chest. "Hey, Issabella, welcome back!" Ishmael's grin stretched wide—too wide—as he stepped inside, his eyes gleaming with excitement. She swallowed the lump in her throat, trying to suppress the unease lingering in her gut. He didn't seem to notice her hesitation.

"What happened?" he asked, concern lacing his voice. "When I woke up, you were still unconscious. I was worried about you." His gaze swept over her, taking in the sight of her sitting upright, the relief on her face too clear to miss. "I wanted you to be comfortable, so I put you in your bed."

Issabella's brows knitted together. Only thirty-three minutes?

She blinked, disoriented. Had it really been that short? The events leading up to her return felt stretched, far beyond what she thought possible. She parted her lips to speak but hesitated, words eluding her. "I thank you, brother," she said at last, her voice quieter than intended. "For making sure I was good."

Ishmael chuckled, his eyes gleaming with an energy that felt just a little too… eager.

"We did it, Issabella. We corrected the mistakes of the past and fulfilled the prophecy Grandmother Eshe gave us." His tone brimmed with triumph, yet something about the moment felt too light. Too easy.

"To God be the glory," Issabella murmured, almost absently, as she ran a hand through her tangled hair.

"Amen," Ishmael replied, his voice too bright, too eager, as if the gravity of the moment had completely escaped him.

"Well, I'm going to shower and wash the sins of the past off my body, then get some rest," he added, his tone still unnervingly cheerful, his presence lingering too close.

Issabella forced a laugh, her thoughts still spinning out of control. "Yes, indeed, brother. I'll do the same." She smiled weakly, but the unease twisting in her gut refused to fade. Something felt off.

As Ishmael turned to leave, exhaustion crashed over her. She collapsed onto her bed, sinking into the soft comfort, her heart still pounding. I made it home. It's over.

But the moment she closed her eyes, the sound of footsteps shattered the silence.

Thud. Thud. Thud.

Her eyes flew open just in time to see Ishmael standing at the foot of her bed again. His grin stretched too wide, a wild gleam flickering in his eyes.

"Quick question, big sister," he said, his voice almost too casual, too smooth. "Where in the hell did you get this apple?"

Before she could answer, Ishmael sank his teeth into it, crunching down loudly. Juice dripped down his chin, spattering onto the floor, his face twisting into an expression of pure, unrestrained pleasure.

"It's literally the sweetest fruit I've ever tasted," he murmured, his eyes gleaming with an unsettling glow. A chill crept down Issabella's spine, stealing the air from her lungs. Ishmael's gaze darkened, shifting into something familiar. Something dangerous. The taste of betrayal clung to her tongue, thick and suffocating. The darkness had already begun to spread.

The End

www.ingramcontent.com/pod-product-compliance
Lightning Source LLC
Chambersburg PA
CBHW070625310726
48982CB00001B/171